D. A Mc

REBIRTH OF BLOOD

The Jessica Dyer Files, Book 1

Rebirth of Blood

Published by David Alfred McCormick.

Copyright ©2021. David Alfred McCormick. All rights reserved. Paperback ISBN: 9798474481128

Hardcover ISBN: 9798484752546

No part of this book may be reproduced in any form or by any mechanical means, including information storage and retrieval systems without permission in writing from the publisher/author, except by a reviewer who may quote passages in a review.

All images, logos, quotes, and trademarks included in this book are subject to use according to trademark and copyright laws of the United Kingdom.

MCCORMICK, DAVID ALFRED, Author REBIRTH OF BLOOD

DAVID ALFRED MCCORMICK

All rights reserved By David Alfred McCormick.

The book is printed in the United Kingdom.

Cover Designed by GetCovers.

Dedication

To Chelsea, Olivia, Iris and Memphis.
You inspired me to never give up, if I hadn't meet you this book would have never been written.

Katie
Thank you for always
Being an insperation,
never stop chasing
your Dreams

From
David Micormick

Table of Contents

TABLE OF CONTENTS 7

CHAPTER 1 1

CHAPTER 2 21

CHAPTER 3 29

CHAPTER 4 55

CHAPTER 5 75

CHAPTER 6 83

CHAPTER 7 93

CHAPTER 8 109

CHAPTER 9 119

CHAPTER 10 133

CHAPTER 11 147

CHAPTER 12 151

CHAPTER 13 159

CHAPTER 14 163

CHAPTER 15 169

CHAPTER 16 173

CHAPTER 17 185

CHAPTER 18 .... **191**

CHAPTER 19 .... **199**

Chapter 1

A little while after breakfast, we rushed from our hotel. Getting on the tour bus, I was as giddy as a kid onChristmas morning. It was the off-season, so it was only my dad and me on the tour. Sitting on the tour with my dad, I was a ball of excited energy, my dad glowed with joy, and our driver was in high spirits. Our tour guide drove towards our destination, regaling us with stories, legends, and fairy tales. I was entranced by his voice. It was hypnotic and just made me melt inside.

"Now, Finn McCool was the son of Cumhull, the leader of the Fianna. He famously and accidentally gained all the knowledge in the world. Can you imagine? I think it would be like having google running in your brain." He let out a Booming infectious laugh and continued his tale. "As I was telling you, there was a magical salmon in the river Boyne that was said to hold all the knowledge of the earth, and our boy Finn was to cook it for the chief poet, Finnegus. But while cooking the fish, Finn burnt his fingers and instinctively put them in his mouth to cool the burn. Unknown to Finn, he had a small amount of the magical fish on his fingers and as it went into his mouth, a light flashed, and Finn instantly knew all about the past present and future." He let the story sink in. I couldn't imagine going from being the simple son of the village chief to being all-knowing. Would people believe him? Would people accept him? Maybe they would shun him from their society? What would it do to his worldview, there were just so many ramifications stemming from such a simple act of burning his fingers? I was staring at the driver, entranced by the lilting brogue of his voice. I think I've finally found the love of my life. I could listen to his voice for hours at a time.

With eyes full of sorrow, I said to my dad, "Just think, if the salmon in the river was real, we might be able to cure mum, and she could come on trips with us again."

Before my dad could answer, there was a loud bang, and the tour bus pulled sharply to one side. I was flung into the side of the bus, and I could see our driver try to regain control. The metal frame of the bus groaned, and I could see the inside of the bus warp as the two ends pulled in opposite directions. Tearing my eyes from the surrounding chaos, I stared at my dad, looking for reassurance that everything would be okay, but all I saw was the look of horror and fear. The bus listed to one side, and I reached for my dad's hand, but it was too late. The bus was flipping, and we were being tossed about like clothes in a washing machine. Being thrown from my seat, I smashed my head against a window panel, and my world went blank. In the space of time that felt like a few seconds but could have been longer, I found myself outside the wreckage of the bus. I ran towards the twisted remains of the wreckage, hoping to find my dad andour drive shaken but alive and well.

A hand grabbed me roughly by the shoulder, trying to restrain me, but I hardly noticed its presence. All I could focus on was the mutilated bus. Then I saw it, my dad's arm hanging out one of the bus's shattered windows. Looking back at the figure trying to restrain me, I noticed he was strangely dressed. "Please," I asked, tears running freely. "My dad is in there. Can you get him and our guide too? They could be injured." The tears obscured my vision as I pleaded with the stranger.

The taller of the two looked down at me. "Why would I help them? They are useless to me. I caused this wreck so I could get to you. Now shut up and stay still while I deal with this wreckage."

I didn't understand what he meant, what he wanted with me, and why he wouldn't help the others. I tried to get up and make my way over to the bus. If they wouldn't help, then I would get them out myself. His short, shabby associate grabbed me and forced me back to the ground. "Master said to stay there." The shabby little man growled at me.

A sudden light bloomed out of nowhere, so I looked to the source, but it was what appeared to be a ball of flame just floating above the tall man's palm. I must be hallucinating because that isn't possible. With a casual flick of his hand, the ball of flame shot towards the bus and enveloped the entire thing in a furious blaze. "Why did you do that, you monster!" I cried at him. I struggled with the man holding me on the ground. The taller man just stared. "I told you to shut up," he yelled. He shoved his aconite aside and lifted me by the throat. "You will learn to obey me in time, or you will end up like your father." He struckme with his other hand and dropped me to the ground. I didn't know if it was the force of the blow or the shock of all that had happened, but it was all enough to knock me unconscious again. As my awareness faded, I could hear my dad's screams of pain.

When I came to, everything was fuzzy. I felt a sharp pain at the base of my scalp. I reached up, thinking Ihad caught my hair in my sleep. What I didn't expect to find were the rough callous hands of someone wrapped in my hair. My eyes flew open in shock. "No, this can't be real. It was a nightmare. Where am I? Please let me go!" I screamed loudly. I struggled to pull myself free from my captor's grip. "Haha… Look, master, sleeping beauty has woken up. Would you like me to quieten her?" That's when I noticed the other man again. "No, Mallory, just bring her. I would like this one to know what I plan to do with her." His voice was that of an over-privileged school boy that had never heard the word no.

"Please. I promise I won't tell anyone what happened, but please just let me go," I pleaded.

"I would say I'm sorry, child, but that would be a lie. I need you for some research, and those I work for are getting impatient with the results. So unfortunately for you, I won't be freeing you."

The horror of my situation truly set in, and I doubled my efforts into resisting Mallory. As I pulled away, trying to get to my feet, he pulled me back, causing me to scream. I was sure he was pulling lumps of hair from my head, but I didn't care. I screamed and fought as hard as I could. I needed to get out. After just a few seconds of my resistance, I felt a slight loosening of Mallory's grip. Thinking that this was my chance, I made to run in the direction we had just come from, but I was too slow. Mallory was instantly on me, hand raised, and he struck with the back of his hand, sending me tumbling into a rough wall. It was then I realised we were in some sort of tunnel or mine shaft. Mallory then had me pinned to the wall, his hand twisting into the fabric of my shirt.

"Now, are you going to behave, or are you going to let me hurt you more?"

I looked him straight in the face and spat the small amount of saliva I had in my mouth at him. "Go fuck yourself, scumbag!" I know it wasn't the smartest thing for me to do, but I couldn't resist. In response, he raised his fist and drove it straight into my solar plexus. This forced me to gasp for air. I noticed as I was coughing and gasping for breath that Mallory was pulling back his arm, readying for another hit. "Enough!" That got both of our attention.

"Mallory, you know better than to let the lab rats get to you. We need them healthy, or there is no point in any of this. I hope you haven't damaged her too badly."

"I'm sorry, master, I didn't mean to disappoint you." If I wasn't so terrified, I would have laughed. Mallory was like a pet dog looking for his master's approval. I would remember that for later. If I lived long enough, it might come in handy.

With his hand still balled in my shirt and my body too weak after his last hit to put up much resistance, he began dragging me in the wake of his master's lead.

It wasn't long before we came to a solid-looking door that seemed to be made from the wall itself. Mallory stopped. I am still gripped tightly in his gorilla-like fist. I watched as his master seemed to draw something in the air. I couldn't make out what it was, but the air seemed to glow where he had drawn it then with a defying groan. I was greeted with an opening that led into pure darkness. My attention was then taken again by Mallory's master, who had muttered something under his breath. I couldn't make out any of the words, but it seemed to be the same chant over and over. Moments stretched by, and that is when I heard it in the darkness. The sound of something solid scraping against the stone and the clanging of some sort of machinery or chains, all this was confusing me where was the noise coming from all I could see was darkness in the room. Then, out of the darkness, I heard the defining roar of something truly terrifying. I, with the little strength I had left, tried to run, but it was futile. Whatever was in there, I knew I wouldn't survive if I came face to face with it. Mallory was laughing at my reaction.

"You shouldn't fear that creature. You should fear my master." He began laughing and pulled me into the darkness with him. His master strode ahead, still muttering under his breath. In an instant, he stopped, and the only thing that could be heard was the distant roar. The door behind us slowly closed. I hyperventilated in panic as we were plunged into absolute darkness, feared had me in its clutches. I couldn't see, and all I could hear was a ferocious roar from some unknown creature. I had to watch as my father had been taken from me. All I knew for sure was that I was in the hands of two mad men who planned to do something horrible to me. I cried uncontrollably, it didn't matter how strong I wanted to be, I just could take anymore. I wanted to wake up, this had to all be a dream.

There was an explosion of light, then we were all

bathing in a warm glow of a blue fire that came from some sort of torch that had been stuck into the surrounding floor. In front of me was my lead captor. He was leaning over some sort of chair that looked like it belonged in a dentist's office for the Middle Ages. Around the chair stood various intravenous poles from which hung dozens of bags of fluid. All the bags had tubing attached that led to various points on the chair.

Roughly shoved into the chair, Mallory held me down as his master cuffed me to the chair. First, he started with my arms and wrists. I struggled, but they were too tight, and I had no wiggle room, so I kicked out, at least trying to injure my captors with my resistance. But it was futile. I was restrained within minutes. The only part of my body I could still move was my neck and head, but this was soon restrained with one leather restraint pulled taught over my neck and another across my forehead. Trying to get some answers, I yelled, "What the fuck are you planning to do to me? If you're just going to killme, get it over and done with." I put as much defiance into my voice as I could, but even to my ears, I sounded defeated.

Mallory's boss turned and regarded me with a genuine curiosity for the first time. "Very well," he said, brushing some stray hair from my eyes as he spoke again. "I don't want to kill you, well, at least not yet. You see, my experiment is very near completion. Just a few more test subjects to survive, and I will showthe lord that his faith in me wasn't misplaced." I wanted to tell him how mad he was experimenting on people in some dank, dark cave but it wouldn't do me any good.

"So, what do you hope to achieve by drawing me here? What are you going to do?".

"I am going to start by giving you an IV, or several, actually, of different compounds that are going to force a change in your body over days and weeks. After every successful course of treatment, I will change the various drugs and compounds, and monitor what these various things do to you. Most don't survive the first few days of the first treatment. But occasionally, I have subjects that live through several treatments. How long do you think you will last?"

There was nothing I could do but accept my fate.

I forgot to mention that between your treatments and my other experiments, you will be a plaything for" Mallory." The shock was too much. I could do and say nothing. They destroyed my life. They took everything away just to make me a thing and an object. Is that all my life boils down to, to be a test subject and play thing for lunatics? I would rather die. But that's when the pain started. I had needles in my arms, legs, neck, and chest, and the fluids got pumped into my body. Whatever was in those IV bags burnt and froze in my veins and muscles without meaning to. I cried out. I tried to stifle it but couldn't. I didn't want these monsters to find pleasure in hearing me scream, but I couldn't stop. The pain was too much. The sounds that came from my throat were unlike anything I had ever heard before. The term blood curdling was the closest description I had for it, but even that wasn't enough. That's when the doorway opened, and I saw them leave like I was nothing. "I hope you survive, I really am looking forward to breaking you." Then they were gone, and I was alone with the strange blue fire burning in their torches and my screams the only company I had.

With my awareness of my soundings fading, I succumbed to the pain as it dragged me into the darkness of oblivion. I heard the rattle of chains and the sound of claws being dragged against the cold and rugged ground. *That's right*, I thought, nearly holding on to consciousness. *I'm not alone in here. They have a monster locked away in here, too.*

My thoughts were interrupted. "Please do not fear me, child." The words posed into my head. I heard them, but not with my ears. It was like a memory of a sound. I tried to call out, but whatever was in those IV bags was making me think too hard. "Who... Are... You?" I mumbled, hoping who or whatever was in here could understand me.

"Please try to stay as calm as possible. I know you are in unimaginable pain, but it's less painful if you stay calm and don't panic."

I tried to turn my head and see whatever was trying to communicate with me, but it was still shrouded in the darkness, so I tried to speak. "I… I.. wi… ll… try…"

"My name is Lyn Saar, and I swear on my blood, I will not leave your side through this ordeal, and I willcall on your ancestors to give you strength as you bear this cruelty. We will watch over you, little one." As she finished speaking, my mind gave out, and it plunged me into the dark and peaceful embrace of unconsciousness.

Unconsciousness couldn't protect me forever. In my brief periods of lucidity, my mind was a maelstrom of pain, rage, and longing for death. I couldn't understand the passage of time between periods of dark oblivion. It could have been hours, days, or months but the periods in my dark refuge became fewer. I fell to the ground, not caring that the rough surface on the cave floor was cutting at my exposed skin.

"I can't be dead. I shouldn't still bleed if I was dead, and I wouldn't still be here. Would I?" I thought aloud that's when I saw the door and I rushed towards it. If I'm alive, I need to get out of here. I need to save my dad. If I could, I needed to get back to my mum. A memory of my mum laying in the hospital bed smiling happily at my reaction when she and dad told me I was getting to go to Ireland pushed me to charge faster. I would get through this door, and I would run as fast as I could out of this nightmare. I was getting close to the door and saw a faint distortion in the air around it, but I didn't care. I charged shoulder first into the door but didn't reach it. I was within inches of impact, and a bright flash like a flare SWAT teams use on tv went off, and I was flung a good 30 feet away from the door. The force of my impact on the solid cave floor was enough to knock all breath from me. I rolled onto my hands and knees, trying to gasp for air. Standing, I screamed, "What the fuck, just let me out! You pricks have had your fun!" The only response I got was silence, so I dropped and just curled up on the floor. Defeated for the moment, I wallowed in self-pity.

I didn't know how long I sat there, but I had cried myself out and had stretched out on the floor just staring at the ceiling. Why me? Why did I have to survive?

Stuck in my head, thinking of all the things that might happen next, and thinking if I will ever get out of this hellhole, I didn't hear the scraping of claws on the rock floor. It was only when that voice hissed quietly into my head that I remembered I wasn't alone

"Hello again, little one, do you remember me?"

"Who are you, and why won't you come out so I can see you?" I slowly stood and tried to gaze into the darkness, just trying to pick up on where this voice was coming from. "If you are with Mallory and his boss, then just stop fucking with me and get on with whatever it is you are supposed to be doing." I had had enough of being toyed with. They were going to do what they wanted, but I didn't have to make things easy for them.

"If you wish to see who I am, I will oblige, but know this, I am not, nor have I ever been in cahoots with Jeremiah or that snivelling creature Mallory."

"So that's the boss's name, good to know. Now, come out so I can see who I'm speaking to."

The sound of chains being pulled along the cave floor and the crunch and scraping of stone under some heave duty claws became louder and louder until the blue light from the torches bathed a dragon in their creepy light. I laughed uncontrollably. "I've lost my mind, I've finally gone crazy that's got to be the answer, the stressed mum being ill, dad being murdered, me being abducted by a bunch of crackpots and being pumped full of goodness knows what for I don't even know how long. And now, I see dragons that can talk in my head. I'm finally having a full-blown breakdown." I huffed, then sat on the floor, crossing my legs, and looked at the dragon.

"That was quite the spectacular tantrum, little one," hissed the dragon in my head. "But I can assure you that I am quite real." I heard a slight grumble coming from the dragon. It took me a second, but I realised it was laughing at me. "The nerve, you think this is funny. I must be the only person in the world that has my hallucination laugh at them."

The deep rumbling grumble continued. "You can think in a hallucination if that helps you, little one." As it spoke, I took a more intense look at it. If nothing else, it was a picture of regal beauty, the scales a purple-grey that reminded me of storm clouds, but they had a pearl-essences shimmer to them, areas of scales seemed to be missing all over its body, then I noticed that as regal as it held itself, it was in poor shape. Scales and claws were missing. It had unmistakable blood stains covering its hide and one of its eyes looked to have a milky white film over it. Who could do this to something so beautiful?

"What happened to you?" I gasped with tears moistening my eyes.

"Little one, you are not that mad mage's only prisoner." It was then that I noticed the manacles on the dragon's legs and one around its neck. "I have been his prisoner for many years. These manacles and chains suppress my power and stop my magic. The way I am now, a hatchling would be strong enough to defeat me in battle."

"So it's hopeless. We can't escape." I looked away. I didn't want this beautiful majestic being to see me cry.

"No, little one, it is not hopeless. You have survived. That in its self is cause for celebration. None have lasted as long as you have. You have an incredible will to survive, and you need that willpower here." "I'm sorry." I wipe my tears away. "I haven't even introduced myself. I'm Jessica, but you can call me Jess."

"Thank you, Jess. I am Lyn Saar, mistress of the sky and storms."

"Could you tell me how long I've been here and what he's planning?

"You have been here for a few weeks, I believe. Most of the previous humans they have brought here have only lasted a few days. A few have lasted a week. In the years he's been doing this, you are the first to ever get released from the chair still alive." She stopped here to let the gravity of her statement sink in. "I believe I know what he is attempting to achieve, but I can't be certain. Long ago, before my great grandparents were even hatchlings, wars ravaged all the realms. Humans, elves, vampires, shapeshifters, harpies, all the fantasy creatures you have ever heard of, and more that you haven't battled for dominance. Some of the older species avoided getting involved with some of those were the watchers, the dragons, and the elementals. But all because they didn't wish to get involved didn't mean they didn't still require people to defend their borders if someone dared to challenge them. So, their solution was to create soldiers they could control. They selected some of the best soldiers in the human realm and performed a ritual to give these soldiers additional power. It involved the blood of dragons being given to these soldiers and a lot of magic to achieve the change. Once completed, the human's strength, speed, intelligence, dexterity, lifespans, and magical power increased dramatically. They also gained some of the innate gifts the Donner of the blood possessed. At first, this solution worked, and everyone was happy with the results. Then something happened. The history here is murky, but it appears the blood worriers led a revolt and tried to take control of all the realms. The war that this caused was the worst ever recorded, and nothing of its equal has been seen since. That was when the council formed each species has its own then representatives from them form the high council. The only power greater than them is the watcher council. The first act of the combined councils was to issue an extermination order for all blood warriors, and the creation of their kind has been outlawed ever since."

"You think he made me one of those?"

"Jess, I honestly don't know. From what I've seen, he can't be doing that, but I can't think of what else it could be. I know he's trying to develop a weapon, but that's all I know for sure."

"Wait, you said that these blood warriors are stronger than most other things, so that means I will get stronger, right?" My face should have given away what I was thinking.

"Not that straightforward, little one. Look at your ankle!"

I did as I was asked, and for the first time, I saw a thin silver band, and it looked like it had some strange writing on it. I looked at Lyn with panic in my eyes.

"What's this?"

"If I had to guess, it's something similar to what he has on me to stop me from escaping."

"Okay, that just means we need to be more creative with our escape attempt." Lyn growled. Then in my head, she said, "He's coming. The chains are pulling me back, so I can't attack."

She then let out a deafening roar, and I looked towards the door, seeing it slowly open. In strode Jeremiah, accompanied by the scumbag Mallory.

"Oh look, master, sleeping beauty is awake." He sounded like an excited child.

"So it would seem, Mallory," said Jeremiah.

Mallory giggled to himself. The sound of it made the hairs on my neck stand on end.

"So Jessica, are you ready to be a well-behaved little girl, or are you going to make me punish you?" Jeremiah asked.

I tried to look confident and even a little defiant. "Why don't you just get over yourself and let me go?" I didn't know where that came from, but it felt good to see him recoil at my defiance.

I could still see the captive dragon, Lyn, try to desperately to break free of her chains, and she roared in her obvious frustration. This was obviously one step of defiance too many as he strode towards me, lifting his hand as he struck me with the back of it to the side of my face, forcing me to stumble and fall to the ground. Then he waved his hand through the air and formed a glowing ball of purple mist. At a silent command, it shot through the air and struck Lyn square in the chest. The mist washed over her body and caused her to let out a bloodcurdling roar. It was the saddest sound I had ever heard, and it broke my spirit to realise just how twisted Jeremiah really was. As the events played out in front of Mallory, he let out more giggles and claps of joy.

"Now, Jessica, come with me quietly, or I will be forced to carry on hurting your friend." As he said this, he raised his hand and formed another ball of mist.

"Okay, please stop. I will do what you asked," I sobbed. I couldn't let her suffer more than she already was, so I got up and followed. That's when I heard Lyn's voice. "Please be brave, my little dragon."

"The things I plan to learn from you will change the world. You're the first step to me realising my dream. If I can unlock the secrets of how you survived, my research will finally be complete. Nothing in history has ever been as special as you are going to be."

He led me out of this part of the cave. I had Mallory following close behind. I tried to look obedient and broken, keeping my head down and my shoulders hunched but still trying to take in my surroundings, trying to make a kind of mental map.

Chapter 2

I kept following, too scared to say anything. Silently keeping track of the twists and turns, I noticed there was a downward incline. I needed to head in the other direction, but I had no way of escaping these crackpots. So I kept following, trying to make myself look weak and timid, hoping that eventually, they would underestimate me. We soon came to a large steel door. It had an electric lock. I couldn't see what he entered into the panel. Once he unlocked the door, it made a grinding noise as the door slid into a recess built into the wall. A plume of dust temporarily obscured my view of what was beyond, but I had a feeling I would not enjoy it once I found out.

Jeremiah was strode in the chamber like a man confident in his surroundings. This was a place he felt comfortable and at home. Seeing that freaked me out, and I was hesitant to follow. Noticing my reluctance, Mallory shoved me forward. "Come on, the master is waiting." I resisted his prompt to move forward, so he pushed harder, making me stumble forward. It was then that I got my first glimpse into the chamber. My blood ran cold as I realised the sort of experiments he was going to perform. In the middle of the room was an operating table. And next to it stood a trolley filled with scalpels and other equipment that I had seen on TV. Lining the walls were dozens if not hundred of specimen jars of varying sizes and shapes filled with limbs and organs, some of which I could identify and others I couldn't. Somewhere full of claws, teeth, and even scales, and in the very centre was an eye. It was displayed front and centre. I freaked out.

Mallory went to shove me further, clearly frustrated that I still wasn't moving. "I said move. We don't keep master waiting. Get on the table now, or I will make you regret it." I hastened to one side as Mallory went to shove me further into the chamber as he let his frustration get to him.

I didn't wait to see what happened. I just took my opportunity and ran. I followed the path that led back to my fellow captive, hoping that I could find a way out from there. I kept heading up, going and praying that I would find an exit soon. At the back of my mind, I was wondering why no one seemed to chase me. It's not like I had much of a head start. Now wasn't the time to worry about that. I came to a split in the path, not thinking. I just followed my instinct and chose the left path. *I hope this is the right one*, I thought, praying that I was out of here soon. It was then that I saw the bright light coming from the end of the tunnel. "Yes, I've found it. I'm finally getting out of here." I quickened my pace. Details of the coast came in to focus, so I pushed myself to go even faster I wouldn't let them catch me, not now. That's when it hit me—pain, the thin shackle on my leg glowed, sending searing pain through my body. I hit the ground with a thud. My body was having some sort of fit or spasm. I couldn't control my movement as my body flailed around. I didn't know how long this lasted. All I knew was that by the time it stopped, I was gasping for air. My throat felt raw from my screams, and my face was wet with shed tears.

Jeremiah knelt in front of me, shaking my face in his hands. "I have let you have your fun. I have allowed you to run around my facility to your heart's content. I did not give chase, neither did Mallory, although I can assure, you he really wanted to. I did this to show you you can not escape me. You are now my possession. You are nothing more than a plaything. Once I am done with you, I will dispose of you. But while you still draw breath, you can never get out of my reach." He then stood, brushing dirt from his clothes. "Now, I have wasted enough time on this ridiculous escape of yours. You will come with me so I can start my work." As he said this, I could see a glint in his eye that told me all I needed to know. This guy was a complete psycho, and he was going to do everything he could to break me.

I didn't move. I just lay there. What was the point if he was just going to kill me anyway? Why should I make it easy for him? "So, you refuse to walk, I see. Well, you leave me no choice." He snapped his fingers, my joints locked and my limbs stiffened. Then he chanted. I couldn't make out the words, but it was almost musical. If I wasn't so angry, I would have laughed. After a few moments of his chanting, he stopped and walked. It was then that I realised I was levitating in his wake. I guess that was one way to get me to comply. It didn't take nearly as long for us to get back to the cave that I had run from. I spotted Mallory sulking in the corner, his rage nearly contained. Jeremiah made a sweeping motion with his hand towards the operating setup, and my body just floated itself into place. I couldn't resist or fight back.

Once on the table, I had restraints applied to my arms, legs, feet, hands, and even neck. Then he released his magic. When he did this, I noticed that holding whatever magic he had used in place seemed to tire him out. That's good. At least his power is finite, I could work with that. I tried to wiggle to see if there was any give in the restrain's, but unfortunately, they were almost as tight as his magic's hold,

"Now we know the dragon can regenerate, but has it passed that ability onto you, I wonder?"

He lifted a scalpel and sliced my filthy clothes off me. In doing so, he was cutting into my flesh. As he pulled the last of my clothing away, he ran fish hands over the wounds, encouraging them to bleed more freely.

Mallory bounced on the balls off his feet, giggling with excitement as his master leans in closer to inspect this own handy work.

"Yes, they are already healing faster than anything I have seen before." He looked me straight in the eye, his face alight with a frenzied joy. "Oh, do you know what this means?" he asked, obviously not wanting a reply. "I've done it, the superiors will be so happy, but now it's time to go get more data." His grin turned more predatory as he moved in closer, scalpel raised, and began cutting. I screamed as his cuts became deeper, and he began carving chunks of flesh and muscles from my arms and legs. They ignored my cries of pain. He just kept cutting and gouging for what felt like an hour. My voice left me long before he was done. All I could do by the end was whimper. Every time a slight gust of air brushed past my exposed injuries, it would feel like every nerve was on fire.

Jeremiah lent close to me. "I hope you enjoyed this as much as I have. Next time, we will see how deep your healing goes. We will see if it's just the flesh or if you can regenerate organs too." He laughed to himself. "Mallory, wheel her back to the dragon. I'm done for now, and ensure you give her more of the solution. Let's see if she can handle more and how it affects her," as he walked out the door. I couldn't hang on any longer, and I passed out, my mind no longer able to endure this treatment.

***

When I came back around, I was back on the cot in the main cavern. Lyns head lay a small distance away from me. Her eyes locked on me. I looked down to assess how bad the damage was and realised I was covered in blood and filth, but as naked as the day I was born. I also had another catheter in my arm connected to an empty fluids bag. What the hell was he pumping into my system? I tried to move, and mybody ached like they had beaten me with a baseball bat.

"Hey Lyn, how long was I out for?"

"He brought you back two days ago. I honestly didn't think you would survive. I am happy that I was wrong. What he did to you is horrific, and I hate that you had to endure it."

"I tried to escape. I got to the entrance, but then I couldn't get any further. I tried, but he wasn't even fazed by it. It was like he found it amusing."

"Thank you for trying. We will bide our time. Maybe they will slip up, and we will escape soon."

"When he took me, he hit you with a spell. He didn't hurt you too badly, did he?"

"No, I was fine within a few hours."

"I'm assuming it was more of your blood in those bags." I pointed to the empty IV bag.

"It was, but if it helped you recover, then I'm happy

to give it."

"The place he took me to was horrible. When you said he was harvesting tissue from you, I did not know how bad it had been. Lyn, I saw your eye in a jar, and he had specimens of body parts and organs. Is that what will end up happening to us? Are we just going to end up dissected and put on display for this psycho's pleasure?" As I finished speaking, I cried. Lyn let me cry for myself. Once the tears stopped, Lyn spoke, "Jessica, I am a dragon and have lived a great number of years, and experienced some truly awful times, some of which have been lost to history. When I was last among my people, I hibernated, unsure if I would ever choose to walk the world again, or if I would take my last sleep. But meeting you in this place has helped me in my decision. I am going to go into the world again and see the realm anew. I will bear this man's ministrations for as long as it takes for us to either escape or be found. Eventually, my presence will be missed in the paranormal world, and I'm sure the authorities will look into your disappearance. Hope is not a lost, child, so please do not give in to despair. We will have to keep lifting each other spiri's, that is the only way we will survive the trials that stand before us." I took a great deal of comfort in what Lyn said. Together, we would fight and we would survive.

The second day of the experiment started the day after I woke. In the hours since I recovered from my first treatment, I only had one visitor other than Lyn. My guest was none other than Mallory, who threw a crusty loaf of bread at me and took the IV equipment with him. "The master will continue his tests shortly." Then, he left.

Chapter 3

"Are you looking forward to today's session?" he asked. I refused to give him the satisfaction and just layon the table, ready to be strapped down.

"Oh, are you not in a talkative mood today? Well, that's okay. I'm sure you'll be vocal eventually. Mallory, strap her down." The snivelling Mallory rushed to my side and strapped me down, muttering to himself about how his master was excited to get some organs from me today. Hearing this sent a chill down my spine. I knew he had said he wanted to cut me open, but he had to be lying. I wouldn't survive something like that.

"Now Jessica, seeing as you 're being so brave, I am going to tell you what I have planned." He was shifting from side to side, itching to get started, but he needed to scare me first. "Now, your cells have gone through some amazing changes, and while you have been recovering, we have been watching you closely, seeing how your muscles and flesh have knitted themselves back together at an incredible rate. There are beings out there that can recover from injuries like you, so I now need to see how much your body can take before it stops recovering." He clapped his hands excitedly. The" first thing I'm going to do is a 'Y' incision, here." He showed on my body where he would cut, trailing his finger along the path his blade would follow. "Then, I need to get past your ribs so I can get to all the nice bits inside you. Now, to do that, I can use this." He picked up a metal contraption that looked like it was a medieval torture device. He placed it carefully back on the table, then lifted an electrical saw. "Or I can use this."

I cried as the genuine horror of what was happening sunk in. "Oh, don't worry, Jessica, I will make sure you live. I want to do this experiment repeatedly. I have to replicate my results now, don't I? But that's only where it begins. Your body can survive so much just being a regular human, but with your healing factor being so strong, I can do so much more. I'm going to take one of your lungs, your kidneys, your spleen, your appendix, your gall bladder. I want to see if you can regrow them. Shouldn't that be fun?" The guy was crazy. But I refused to give him the satisfaction of knowing I was scared.

He started his first cut, and I felt my stomach recoil at the wet feeling of my blood soaking my chest. I gritted my teeth, refusing to scream, but could do nothing to stop myself from hyperventilating. It didn't take him long to finish the first series of cuts. That's when the real pain started. He peeled the top flap of skin up over my chest, exposing my ribs. I was sobbing uncontrollably. Was my resolve this weak?"Now, that's the reaction I wanted. This is beautiful," he said while staring into my chest. He then started the saw, and as I saw it creep towards my chest, my mind went blank. I was gone, and he couldn't hurt me if I blacked out. I didn't care what he did to my body. I would either recover, or I would die.

After a few sessions in the lab, I was not proving to be the test subject my captor was hoping for. Every time he started his experiments, I would blackout because of the pain, so after half a dozen sessions with him, I was expecting to see his usual sour-looking face when he came to escort me from my cave- dwelling with my dragon compatriot, but this time he looked at me with a look of pure insanity. "Don't worry, precious, you won't escape me today. I have lots of delicious treats in store for you."

He let out a cackle that chilled me to the bone, but I refused to show him my fear. It's what he got off to, and I refused to give him the pleasure. So I was led to the room of my nightmares. Once we were there, I was forced to lie on the cold, hard table. By now, I was used to the fact that I hadn't been given a stick to wear. Once Mallory had strapped me down to his satisfaction, he whispered close to my ear, "No escape for sleeping beauty today. I hope he will let me have a turn."

I didn't think it was possible, but at that moment, I varied. I was in a nightmare. I hoped I would wake up staring at Lyn, shaken but relieved it wasn't real.

Jeremiah looked over the restraints, making sure they were fully secure. *That's weird. He never does that.* He then reached into his pocket and pulled a syringe full of a green liquid. The colour and consistency reminded me of dish soap.

"No more passing out for you," he said in almost a singsong way as he violently jabbed the needle into me.

"Ouch, that hurt, asshole," I screamed. I couldn't believe I had just said that. All colour drained from my face when I saw the look of pure rage cross his face.

"Well, aren't you a mouthy little lab rat today. I was going to wait till later, but I think I'll do it now. Yes, now will be good. Maybe it will teach you who is in charge around here," Jeremiah muttered to himself, as though talking himself into doing something that even he knew was wrong. I was in a pure state of fear. I hadn't had to endure his ministrations because I always passed out, I have only had to deal with the after-effects and my mind has been in a state of unconsciousness until my body repairs itself. Now, I will endure it I have to.

"Now, I'm going to show you just what a little slut does." He took his clothes off, and my heart rate went through the roof as I realised just what he was planning to do. My panic overrode my senses, and I thrashed in my bindings as I struggled. Mallory watched in fascination, clapping and cheering like it was some sort of sick sport.

***

By the time he had finished, I was a broken mess. I don't remember how I got back to the cave that Lyn and I were held in, but I realised soon after getting there that Lyn was projecting a calm feeling towards me and telling me we would be okay. As I took note of my condition, I realised I was in worse shape than I can ever remember being in. I had another IV line giving me more of what I could only assume was more of Lyn's blood. Beside me sat a bowl of some stew and some bread. I tried to move, and pain shot through my body,

"Try to move as little as possible. You need to stay as still as you can so the bones can set right."

Bones, I thought, then memories came flooding back. After he raped me, he broke my bones in slow, calculated ways. He started with my legs, breaking them in several places, then cutting away the flesh and muscle tissue so he could watch in real-time as they repaired themselves. He was so excited hearing me scream in pain as he watched my bones knit themselves back to gather. I thought I was going to go crazy. The constant breaking of bones and the slicing of skin were sickening. I wept and screamed as he continued his observations. When he got bored with breaking my legs, he moved on to my left arm. He started with my fingers first, dislocating them and timing how long it took them to heal. Then he broke them with different objects, seeing which did more damage or what types of breaks took longer to heal.

"Lyn, how often do they change the IV bag after they bring me back here?" I asked. I had a plan. I was getting out of here, even if it killed me. "I think every few hours. The bag doesn't stay empty for long," Lyn explained, her head tilted to one side like she was trying to see what I was planning in my head.

"The bag is about halfway done. I assume they give it to me to speed the recovery so they can run their experiments more frequently," I said, thinking out loud.

"I think you 're right, but how does that help us now?" Lyn asked, clearly not following my train of thought.

"Can your teeth or claws cut through a bone?" I asked.

"Yes, they can, but it will hurt. How do you plan on getting out?"

"When Mallory comes to change the IV bag, I'm going to kill him." My voice was bitter and detached. They weren't people, they were scum, and I had no problem with ridding the world of them.

***

The time had come. Lyn had removed the band of silver from around my ankle. It wasn't as straightforward as I had hoped, but we managed it. Whatever Jeremiah had given me to remain conscious was still in effect, so I had to endure the iron tear and bite through bone, flesh, and muscles, but it would be worth it. I then crawled towards where the cave entrance always appeared and waited for my prey to arrive whole I regrew that part of my leg.

By the time Mallory arrived, my leg hadn't completely regrown, but that was okay. I was leaning against the wall for support. As he walked in, he didn't notice that I wasn't there. He was too busy muttering to himself.

"Maybe next time, master will let me have a turn. I want to make her cry too." *I'm definitely doing the world a favour by killing this creep.* I swung the IV pole as hard as I could into the side of his head. Shocked by the amount of damage that I inflicted, he hit the floor hard, but I could see he was still breathing. I crawled to where his body had fallen,n drawing the pole with me and beating at his head until all that was left could only be described as mince meat. I doubt his ass could heal from that. I crawled towards the doorway and shouted to Lyn, "I will be back for you."

"Go before it's too late."

I made my way out, trying to remember the fastest route from my first escape attempt. It didn't take long for me to find the right path, and I tried to push past the pain in my leg. *This is nothing. I can endure it.* I chanted this as a mantra, pushing myself further. Then, I made it. I was out. I was free. The shock stopped me for a moment as I took in the blue sky, the waves from the ocean, the smell of them was so refreshing. That is when I heard it— the slow applause— *clap, clap, clap*.

"Well done, Jessica. I would have never thought you would be capable of such a thing. I have definitely underestimated you and the dragon, but don't worry, that won't happen again." I turned my head to see Jeremiah leaning on the rock face just off to the side of the entrance like nothing important had happened and he was just having a pleasant discussion. Then I saw the ball of energy that was floating above his hand.

"Now, I'm going to have to punish you for killing my servant." He then threw the energy ball at me. When it struck, I was out like a light.

***

Lyn and I then developed a routine. Jeremiah would come experiment on one, if not both of us. He would rape me, trying to break my spirit, then he would leave us. Every day, I would receive a bowl of stew and some bread, and once a week, Druk would get two butchered cows. When we were alone, Lyn would tell me about the paranormal world, the other realms, and the creatures that inhabited them. I was hooked on every detail Lyn told me—I couldn't get enough. The evenings spent learning from my new friend made the days with Jeremiah more tolerable, but I found that the longer it went on, the worse he got. Over time, he removed limbs to see if they would grow back. These days would be followed by me being restrained in my cot in the cave, watching as he experimented on Lyn. Time passed slowly here. I never knew if it was days or weeks that passed over time. I noticed I was getting taller, and my figure was changing. I wasn't sure if this was because of the constant IVs I was getting of dragon's blood or because I was getting older, but I wasn't just changing in appearance; I was getting more confrontational and less meek. Jeremiah frequently punished me and made his experiments more extreme when I talked back to him.

Now and then, he chained me to the cave walls and floor like he did with Lyn, so we couldn't interfere when he dragged in a new test subject. He would make us watch as they writhed in agony as the blood would work into their system. Most didn't even last 24 hours.

One day, after a bad experience in the lab, I was sitting propped against Lyn's front legs. It had become my favourite place to sit and feel comfortable. While I was relaxing, trying not to think of what I hadbeen put through, Lyn was projecting images of her flying past snow-capped mountains.

"So, what did you do to make him remove your fingers and break your toes?"

I laughed. The memory of his face contorted in rage was right up there in entertainment.

"Well, after he was done enjoying himself, I realised that one of my hand restraints had come loose, so I may have thrown something at his dick and given him the finger. He was not as amused with my shenanigans as I was. So, as a punishment for damaging his cock, he broke my toes with a hammer. Can you believe it? He smashed each of them one at a fucking time, and I can tell you, that shit hurts. I was feeling a little bratty, so I laughed at him again. I may have also goaded him and said, if you have finished with my pedicure, I'm overdue for a manicure." I let my statement sink in, and the image of him staring at me was too much. I broke down, clutching my ribs with my stumpy hands as I cried with laughter. "Maybe it was unwise, because then he decided I didn't need my fingers for a while."

As I was telling my story, I could feel Lyn's chest vibrate. She was finding it funny as well. At least someone enjoys my humour.

"So, what warranted such an outburst? You rarely lash out without reason." I took a breath.

"While he was doing his business, he said just think how proud my mother would be that she raised a freak slut. After that, I just wanted to hurt him even though I knew he was going to punish me after." Before Lyn could say anything more, we felt a huge tremor through the cave. Lyn instantly shielded me from any debris that may have come down from the ceiling. As we listened, there seemed to be some commotion outside. I heard screams and explosions going off. Maybe this was it, someone had finally found us. I didn't want to get my hopes up, but what else could it be?

The door leading out of the cave opened, and Jeremiah came charging in, discharging balls of energy behind him at a force of people all dressed in some black tactical gear. The first thing I noticed was that no one carried a gun. A few of them held staffs, a couple had swords and daggers, and others were wielding some energy like Jeremiah.

One individual dressed in combat clothes stepped into the cave. He had an air of confidence that I had never seen before. He was holding an orb of what looked to be red energy, and he spoke in a forceful tone.

"Jeremiah Hind, you are under arrest. Stop resisting, or we will detain you with force."

"If you think you can take me, you are dumber than you look. I have dragon blood in me. I am powerful. Now, come and show me your force, and I will show you how weak you really are."

Jeremiah was defiant. The man who commanded Jeremiah to surrender made a gesture for the rest of his team. It looked like he was telling them to stand down. They all took a few steps back to give him some room.

"Tell you what, Jeremiah. If you can defeat me, the team will let you go free as a bird."

Jeremiah didn't even think about it. He rushed the man, throwing balls of energy as he charged. The man didn't flinch, didn't miss a beat at all. He dodged every blast of energy and stepped out of the way just in time to avoid the physical attack Jeremiah had aimed at his solar plexus. He moved with the grace that most professional dancers would be envious of. As he dodged Jeremiah's attack, he pivoted on one foot while whipping the other around. I could barely see the moment of impact. But when he did make contact with the rib cage, I heard the audible crack of ribs breaking, and the resulting scream that came from Jeremiah told us all who the winner was.

"Get him into restraints. He won't be down for long."

At his command, the rest of the team sprang into action, ensuring they secured Jeremiah in similar, if somewhat smaller, restraints to the ones that held Lyn. He began making his way, too drunk, and his pace was slow and steady. He removed his helmet and face coverings, showing us a handsome face. He had a five o'clock shadow, piercing blue eyes, a nose that looked like someone had broken it a few times, and his lip quirked at the corner, giving the impression that he would be quick to smile. I also thought I saw a few laughter lines in the crease of his eyes.

He reached us and first greeted Lyn. "Lady Saar, I am Commander Robinson. We will have you out of these shackles as soon as possible. We also have healers waiting on standby for you."

"Thank you, Commander. I appreciate your concern for my well-being, but I am more worried about my comrade. This is Jessica, and she requires urgent medical aid. She shouldn't be forced to walk, as he broke all her toes earlier today, and she will not be questioned until I am with her. Do I make myself clear, commander?"

"Yes, ma'am. I will retrieve the healers immediately. I will also get a team working on your restraints." He rushed out of the cave, barking orders at everyone as he passed.

"Lyn, that wasn't very nice. I think you scared that man half to death."

"Really, I didn't notice. That being said, you should have been his top priority. As far as he knows, you are a human girl who has been the prisoner of that lunatic, but no, he comes over and tries to fawn over me like I'm some injured kitten. The nerve of some people."

It looked like someone had rubbed her the wrong way, so she was asserting her dominance to show everyone that being a captive hadn't broken her. "Anyway, I wanted to talk to you before they ask questions about what happened. I need you to let me handle everything, and do not leave my side unless I tell you to do so."

"Lyn, you concern me. Aren't these the good guys?"

"You need not be concerned. We just need to tread carefully until we know what's going on and who's pulling the strings. Once we know who these people are and who they report to, we will know how much to disclose."

"Okay, I trust you, and I will follow your lead, but can you try to find out about what happened to my father, and can you find out about my mum?"

"Child, I will find out what happened to both of them, and if they still live, I will move heaven and earth to reunite you with them. Now, let's put our game faces on. He's coming back, and remember, I will do all the talking."

I nodded at her statement, not wanting to disappoint her. Commander Robinson was rushing towards us now with a team of people who all looked flustered.

"Well, Commander, are your people going to treat my comrade? I assume this is also the team to free us from these chains."

At her last word, she shook her gigantic frame, letting the chains clink together to enhance her statement.

***

Within hours, I was patched up. Whatever magic they used was amazing. I was worn out, but my fingers were back on, and my toes were no longer broken. My restraint bracelet had been removed, and I felt like I was walking on air. As per Lyn's instructions, I avoided taking as much as possible, and when asked a question, I kept my answers as short as humanly possible. After my treatment was complete and I was released from the healer's care, I made my way back to Lyn. They were having a little difficulty removing the chains that held her, but as I got near, I saw the last cuff hit the floor.

"That feels so much better. It has been too long since I had a good stretch."

At this, she shook and stretched. It reminded me of how a house cat stretches when they wake up from a nap in a sunny spot. She even stretched her talons and left gouges in the solid rock beneath her.

With Jeremiah detained and denied access to his magic and having her bindings removed, Lyn felt her power rush back to her, embracing her like an old friend.

Before much more happened, the outline of Lyn's body shivered and faded. In her place stood a strikingly beautiful woman. She only looked to be in her late twenties, early thirties, but after spending so much time around her, I knew she was much older snice to be in my human form again now, child. Come here so I can

43

hold you. I have dreamt of "It" comforting you from the day I met you, and I will be denied no longer."

I rushed into her embrace, nearly knocking us both to the ground as she held me. I heard her speak to the commander.

"Yes, Commander, I understand you wish to know what has happened, but as I have said to you repeatedly, we are leaving. You can provide an escort, but we are going to a hotel. We are going to bathe, we are going to eat, and we might even get some new clothes because I don't think the locals will approve of our current attire." At this point, I realised for the first time that Lyn and I were both naked. Lyn noticed me blushing and said to the stunned commander,

"Also, do you have anything that we could wear to the hotel? I would rather we not check in naked." Once everything was taken care of, we dressed in some spare combat clothes and were escorted to the Aurora lodges, where the extraction team had set up a base of operations.

***

At the lodge, we were taken to a beautiful cabin. We insisted we stay together, which caused the commander to grumble. I think he was hoping to get me alone so he could interrogate me. Lyn insisted I clean up and get some rest while she tried to contact some people she knew that would help us. I wasn't overly concerned, and

I rushed to the bath area of my room, where I found a beautiful silver freestanding bathtub and a pile of the softest white fluffy towels I had ever seen. Just looking at the tub and the towels nearly brought me to tears. I took a deep calming, breath and ran one of the hottest bubble baths I could ever remember taking. I spent so long in the tub, scrubbing every single inch of my body, trying to decontaminate myself from the memory of every place he had touched. I scrubbed myself until it hurt. Once I was satisfied that I was clean, I emptied the tub and ran a fresh one so I could relax and try tothink of what my life would be like now. As I lay there in the warm water, the scent of lavender filling theair from the bubble bath I had used, I thought about what was to come next. I knew I had been held captive for a long time, but I honestly didn't know just how long it had been, how much would have changed in that time, if my dad was really dead. And what about my mum? Had she survived her treatment? Where would I go, where would I live? The unanswerable questions kept spinning around my head, and I cried softly, laying there in the warm water. I cried for the longest time, wallowing in my grief until I noticed the water in the tub had become cold, and I was shivering again. I exited the tub, trying to fortify myself. I had my breakdown, now I needed to put on a brave face and take on the challenges that would come at me. But first, a nap. I was allowed a nap, Lyn said so, and nothing was taking a nap away from me. I had earned it. So I wrapped up in the extremely fluffy towel and I made my way to the bed and crawled under the duvet. I had missed duvets, how they hugged and protected you.

I fell asleep the instant my head hit the pillow, and thankfully, it was a dreamless sleep. When I woke, I saw the sun rising from the window, and could hear a heated conversation from the next room and the delicious smell of food cooking. My stomach let out a growl that told me it was demanding food. I chuckled to myself and looked around the room. There was a pile of clothes and pair of boots sat on a chair beside the bed. On top was a note saying I hope these are to your liking. I dressed quickly and looked at myself in the mirror. The clothes and boots fit really well, and I looked good in them. Stone- washed jeans, a long-sleeved black shirt, a pair of timberland boots in black and a long sweeping cardigan. The only thing wrong with the image I saw when I looked in the mirror was the length of my hair. I needed to get it cut, and I looked older. My features were more pronounced, my eyes were brighter.If I didn't know better, I would say I was looking at someone else.

Before I put much more thought into it, I headed out the door of my room to see what all the commotion was and to hopefully get some food.

Walking into the main room of the cabin, my eyes went straight to Lyn. She was dressed in a similar styleto me, but she radiated confidence and power. Across the room from her seated Commander Robinson. He had some other rather grumpy official with him that didn't look happy to be here. Next to Lyn sat a man with a smile, while the other man looked less than impressed about being here, the gentleman who sat with Lyn looked practically overjoyed.

Lyn's voice was dominating the conversation. "I'm not saying you can't speak to Jessica. I am saying you can not hold her responsible for something that was done to her unwillingly. I can testify that she has no sign of dragon madness, and as I have already told you, she is under protection by both the dragon and elf council. I have given you my statement of events. I would rather you not question Jessica, but if you insist, then so be it. Now, will you both be joining us for breakfast, or do you have somewhere else to be?"

The man that was sat with Commander Robinson stood abruptly and excused himself while Commander Robinson remained seated. After a tense few minutes, the commander spoke, "Well, that went better than expected. So, what's for breakfast?" The three of them broke down laughing when I cleared my throat to announce that I was in the room. They all looked at me, and Lyn said, "Ah, little dragon, I should explain, but let's do it over breakfast."

As we all approached the dining table, a woman who looked a little older than me told me to make myself comfortable. We sat at the table. I sat as close to Lyn as I could, still looking to her for protection and guidance. The commander and mystery gentleman were

47

kind enough not to comment about my behaviour. Lyn made introductions.

"Gentlemen, this is Jessica Dyer. You have been told who and what she is, and while I make introductions, I would ask that you hold back on questions." As she spoke, the men nodded in agreement. "Jessica, let me first introduce Commander Killian Robinson. He runs a joint task force between the paranormal military and the paranormal investigation agency. Our other guest, this is Alexander Elric. He is the head of the paranormal investigation agency. Now, Alexander is an ancient friend of mine, and is a member of the elves council and has vouched for you."

At this, I interrupted, "I'm sorry, I don't understand. Why do I need to be vouched for, and what was that other man so angry about? Please, will someone tell me what's happening?"

With a sigh, Alexander held up his hand, and we all went silent. "Child, allow me to explain. Lyn has informed us you know some of our histories but has left out certain things. One thing she hasn't told you is that the joint councils made a treaty a very long time ago in the age when my grandparents were still young. This treaty states that any who dabbled in the ancient blood magic making a blood-born would be sentenced to life in Tartarus. Tartarus is a paranormal prison located under the earth. It is one place all of our kind fear, but that wasn't all that was agreed upon. While the guilty party would be prisoner, the experiments would be destroyed."

I looked around, and all three looked solemn. "Does that mean you are going to kill me?"

Alexander shook his head. "Child, we are not going to kill you. You see, the paranormal world has changed and evolved a lot since then, but we are still concerned with the risk you present. You see, we elfhave known the secret for how to create dragon blood warriors, and it has been a secret that has been verywell guarded. Only a few of my kind know that the knowledge still exists, so while you slept, I examined Jeremiah's workspace in those caves. I also spoke with him and I examined you." I flinched when he said this. "Don't fear, I did not touch you, and I did you no harm, but what he did to you is not make you one of the dragon blood. Only the people in this cabin are aware of this, and we will not make that information public. What he has done can not be explained, but you have the blood and genetic markers for many types of supernatural beings inside you. From what I could sense, he has mainly manipulated your DNA with that of dragon, but I also feel feline shifter DNA and that of the mages. There are others included, but those are the dominant ones."

It stunned me. "So what does that mean? What's going to happen to me, are you going to lock me up and experiment on me like he did?" As I asked this, my breathing quickened, the world was turning fuzzy,and I could not focus heat like energy was running through my body. Lyn and Alexander rushed to my side and held my hands. Both seemed to project calmness the way Lyn would if Jeremiah had left me in astate where I felt more broken than normal. As I calmed down, things refocused. I looked down to where my hands were being held and saw electricity playing over my hands and fingers. It was running up my arms. Lyn and Alexander released my hands, and the energy continued to punch and zip around my handsand arms. I looked at Lyn and she had a look of pride.

"How do I make it stop?" I asked, directing my question to the room at large.

Lyn spoke quietly as though trying not to scare me. "Just close your eyes and focus on your breathing. Asyou breathe in, imagine you are breathing in the energy like it's a part of you."

I did as she said, and in a few breaths, I felt the energy absorb into me, and I felt exhilarated.I opened my eyes and found everyone staring at me. They all looked impressed.

The woman who was cooking up breakfast was standing there with a grin and said, "That is impressive for the first time." She then clapped and announced, "Breakfast is served."

The table shimmered, then groaned as food suddenly appeared, and it all looked mouth-wateringly delicious. With the appearance of food, everything else was forgotten. It was the most impressive breakfast ever. I ate more than I remember ever eating before, and I was probably making myself look like a glutton, but no one seemed to care, so we all continued. Once all the food had been consumed, which took a short amount of time, the woman who I didn't have the pleasure of meeting yet clapped, and the dishes had gone to be replaced with steaming pots of tea and coffee. I couldn't help myself. I said with a grin, "That was amazing. I would love to know how you did it."

"Oh, that was nothing. I'm Minerva, but everyone calls me Mini."

"Hi Mini, I am Jessica."

Alexander cleared his throat to get everyone's attention again.

"Jessica, I have a proposal for you. At the agency we have a training programme. It will help you adjust to your new worldview, and will give you somewhere to call home. It will also mean that you are under the protection of the agency. The reason I brought Mini with me is that she is also in the training programme, and if you accept my offer, I have asked her to be a mentor to you. She will be someone you can talk to a confide in. Is that something that may interest you?"

I thought about what he was offering. It sounded too good to be true, but what was my other option, being made some lab rat? Without thinking I asked,

"What do you get out of this? Why help me?"

Mini laughed without restraint, and the rest of the table all smiled.

Once the table regained its composure, Alexander answered, "That is a simple answer in a few regards. One, my friend asked me to help you and I am happy to help her. Two, I have a feeling that you will be anasset to our team. Three, I don't like the potential to be wasted and I can see that you have great potential. Does that answer your question?"

I replied a little sheepishly, "Yes, it does, and I would be happy to accept your offer. I have one more question. Has anyone been able to track down my mum and dad? How long did Jeremiah hold me captive?"

There was a pregnant pause, and for a moment, I thought my question would go unanswered, then the commander stood and approached me, kneeling to bring himself to my eye level.

"I was hoping to give you good news, Jessica, but I have looked into it personally. You have been in that cave for five years. I have spoken to Lyn, and we understand if you find that hard to believe, but you had had periods after Jeremiah had experimented on you where you would be in a coma for days and weeks. This has given you a skewed view on how much time has gone by. Also, I regret to inform you that your father and your tour guide have both been confirmed dead. Until we located you in the cave system, you were classed as missing, presumed dead as no corpse was found in the wreckage of the tour bus." Although I expected the news, I was still holding out hope he had survived by some miracle.

Trying to hold back my tears, I asked, "What about my mum? She was getting cancer treatment at theRoyal Marsden hospital. She wasn't in great condition. Do you have any news about how she's doing?" "I'm sorry, but after the news that you had both died, she stopped her treatment and passed a few weeks after you and your father were pronounced dead."

I looked at him blankly for a moment, then my new reality set in on me. My last slim line of hope that I had been holding on to was cut away. I was now adrift in an unknown life. It had been five years, even if I tried to rejoin the world and pick my life up where I had left it, nothing would be the same. I wasn't the same girl anymore, I couldn't even really call myself a girl anymore. I was now a woman. I felt a stray tear fall on my cheek and before I knew it, I was in Lyn's arms. She was holding me as if one more shock would break me. Maybe she was right, but right now I had made my decision and it was time to move on.

Chapter 4

"So, Alexander, do I call you sir or anything like that?"

"No, Alex will be fine, although I'm sure some other recruits have more colourful names for me and the other instructors." Mini blushed and quickly looked the other way.

"So, when do we leave?" I asked, looking to Lyn for reassurance.

"We will leave shortly, although Lyn won't be joining us."

I looked up into her eyes and saw the sorrow there. "Unfortunately, I have been away from dragon society for a little too long, and I need to make my presence felt before any get the wrong idea." At the last part of her statement, I'm sure I heard the undertone of a growl, but I couldn't be sure. She lent down and kissed my forehead. "Child, I won't be gone long. You will see me again, and if you need me, Alexander will let me know. Now, my dear one, make me proud."

Lyn walked out of the cabin, and I felt a pulse of energy. I looked round, and Mini told me in a whisper that was her changing her shape into her dragon self. I was taken aback. This would take some getting used to.

I have a car" So what happens now?" I asked to the room at large. The commander answered first." waiting for us outside that is going to take us to the airport, where we have a private jet waiting to take us to the agency's training facility I would advise you rest while you can on the flight, because we are going to hit the ground running with your training."

One week after my arrival, and I could say the commander's statement was not an exaggeration. We trained for 16 hours a day to build my fitness level. This included everything from running on a treadmill, using weights, practicing basic martial arts then ending my day with more running. Every night this first week when I finally got back to my room, I passed out. Apart from my instructors, the only other person I had seen had been Mini. She kept giving me words of encouragement and supported me the first night after training when I said it was too hard and I might as well just assist myself to being a lab rat. That night she gave me a real hard taking to. She also told me that as part of her gifts being a witch, she was an empath and could pick up on my feelings and emotions. She told me she knew I was more than the weak little girl I was acting like, and I needed to be the strong force woman that Lyn believed in and fought to protect. After that rousing speech, I couldn't just back down, so every day since, I was giving 100 percent. The second week of training started the same as the first, but about 14:00, just after I was done with basic martial arts I was called to Alexander's office. As soon I was told, I headed there at top speed hoping to have some information from Lyn. I got to his door and bought my breath before knocking quietly.

"Come in."

"Hi Alex, you sent for me?"

"Yes, Jessica, thank you for coming so quickly. Please take a seat. I have some things I would like to discuss with you."

"Of course, have I done something wrong?"

"No, you are doing brilliantly, and that's what I need to speak to you about."

I must have given him a look of total confusion because he looked concerned when he continued.

"You have been progressing a lot faster than we ever expected you to. The training you completed in the last week is what we would usually put some of graduating teams through, but you seemed to complete it in your stride. How are you feeling at the end of each day and the start of the next?"

"Well, I'm finding the training hard, but I guess I expected that, and by the end of the day, I'm completely wiped out. I usually eat and pass out. As for the next day, I feel great, and I'm eager to start, although I thought I would learn about the paranormal world as well, I just seem to do physical trainingso far."

"Yes, there is a good reason for that. As you can imagine, living in the paranormal world can be physically more demanding than what you are used to, so our initial plan was to get you up to a level of physical strength before we started anything else. We expected it to take quite a while for you to reach the level required to carry on, but you have exceeded our expectations by a very large margin, so what I would like to do is change the plan for you. We will still do physical training and the intensity of it will increase, but the duration will be less. So going forward, the first part of your day will revolve around the physical aspect of training. We are also going to be introduced to weapons training to see what style best suits you. Your afternoons are going to be split after lunch, to give you some breathing space between physically straining forms of training. The first part will be about our history and culture. Once you have a good grasp on that, this will lead into other subjects, like demonology. I will be overseeing your education for this part of your day. The next part of your day will be figuring out your abilities, and Commander Robert is going to help you explore this part of yourself. I will warn you now the workload you are going to undertake is going to be extreme. I would also like to set up a fortnightly meeting between you, your instructors and I so that we can discuss any problems you may be having or any concerns we may have. Does all this sound good to you? I want to have your okay before we go ahead with this. If you don't feel ready yet, we can revisit this conversation in a few more weeks."

He lent forward, looking at me as though he was considering something of great importance and the way I acted would have far-reaching ramifications. I cleared my throat and said,"Yes, that sounds amazing. When do we start the new programme?"

"You will start it tomorrow. Take the rest of the day off. Hang out in the rec area or something, just try to relax. I believe Mini is around if you want some company."

"Thank you, Alex. I really appreciate everything you're doing for me."

***

My time in the gym, although harder than it had ever been, had turned out to be the easiest part of the day. The workouts were extreme. We dropped doing a lot of the cardio and settled more on weight training. This also involved sparring practice, which was becoming the worst part of my day. A few weeks into my new routine, my gym instructor, Hargreaves, said once we did the morning warm-ups, he had something fun for me to play with. I was chomping at the bit to find out what he had planned. He loved to torment me like this, so once we had finished our warm-up—that included a five-mile run on the treadmill and a 30-minute yoga routine—he escorted me past the usual gym that had the hardcore weights in. We passed a few doors that had no sign of what they contained. The suspense was killing me, but I knew Hargreaves would not spoil his surprise. We then left the gym complex through an exit that I didn't know existed and entered another building that was across the yard. It had guards stationed at the entrance, so I had never been in there, and I had never taken much interest in it because I was usually too tired or too busy to care. With practiced motions, the guards waved us in. Once inside, I could feel the excitement radiating from Hargreaves. "Are you ready, kid?"

I had no idea what to expect, so I just nodded, and he let out a hearty laugh. "Laugh it up, big guy. I'll get my revenge when we spare later." This statement just made him laugh louder than ever. "Come on, the surprise is just through that door, and it's also today's lesson."

I looked at two heavy steel doors that he pointed out, and he motioned for me to open them, so bracing myself, I pushed at the doors and realised they were heavier than expected, so I gritted my teeth and put a little more power into my thrust and the doors opened with a groan. Once opened, they stayed that way. "Impressive, those are testing gates. If you can't get through them, it's usually straight back to training. only a few can do it on their first try, but I knew you could do it, kid." He ruffled my hair the way an uncle would to their favourite niece or nephew.

I blushed a little at this act of affection. "Now, come on. Let me show you around. This is the weapons testing and training facility." As I let my eyes wander, I saw a different target setups. There was a traditional shooting range, but also what looked like an archery set up and other sorts of weapons target set ups. I looked at Hargreaves, and he was smiling from ear to ear at my reaction. "Wow, this is awesome, so where do I start?" I just wanted to get out of there and try something.

"Well, let's just go through a few things. First, you can use this facility in your down time if you want to get a little extra practice in. Second, you will still be required to do physical training. The sort of work we do isn't just about using weapons. We must become weapons if the situation requires it. Third, this facility is six levels up and six down. The lower levels are for research and development, so you probably won't need to go down there soon. They are very protective of their projects. The upper six floors are pure weapons training grounds, and the first floor is for ranged weapons, second and third are mid-ranged weapons and the final two are close ranged combat. I have a feeling I know where your talents are going to lie. But today, I have you all to myself. Your instructors have agreed to give you the day off so we can see where your strengths and weaknesses are with weapons. Also, as we explore and try different things, I want you to keep an open mind." As he was talking, I was nodding in agreement, but deep down I was feeling very apprehensive. I had never handled a weapon of any description before and the prospect of something as dangerous as a weapon in my hands was kinda terrifying. "Come on, let's go to the quartermaster."

As Hargreaves continued to explain about different weapons that he would show me today, my focus was drawn to the weapons cage where a tank of a man stood. He seemed to expect our arrival.

As we arrived, the quartermaster greeted Hargreaves. I assumed they were old friends by the way they embraced. "So, you must be Jess. Hargreaves has told me a lot about your progress and I've arranged a few toys for you to try out. Now, am I right in thinking that before you arrived here, you've had zero contact with weapons?" I nodded my agreement to nervous to articulate a response. "That's good, it means we don't need to train out any bad habits and we can teach you the most efficient ways to handle your weapons. So I've been told you are fairly strong, so we don't really need to worry about recoil on firearms so that's what I would like you to start with today. I have a few sidearms and shotguns. How do you feel about trying them?"

"I can give them a go, but I am a little apprehensive

about them."

"It's good to be apprehensive of them. It will make sure you treat them with the care that is required."

He then led Hargreaves and me over to a section of a shooting range with a multitude of targets already set up. Through the entire exchange between the quartermaster and I, he had stayed silent, and it didn't look as though he had any plans of speaking soon, meaning I was purely in the quartermaster's hands.

We stopped at a bench that was set up in front of the target area, and arranged in front of me were three shotguns and three handguns were. Seeing them gave my stomach a nervous lurch. This is getting real, real fast.

"We are going to see how you get on with the shotguns first, lass. Now, from right to left, we have the tabor TS-12 gauge rotating tube-fed semi-auto shotgun, it holds 4 shells per tube, 3 tubes with one shot. In the pipe manual, left or right rotation. Next, we have the DP-12 pump action double barrel rear-loading shotgun with a 16 shell capacity, and finally, the KSG pump action with a max capacity of 14 shells. Then the handguns we have, first up is the HK45 tactical, holds ten-rounds per magazine and one in the barrel has a three-dot sight system and weighs 27.68 ounces empty and fires .45 calibre. Next, there is the sig M11-A1 9mm has a three-dot adjustable sight system, is designed for conceal carry, holds 15 rounds and one in the barrel and weighs 32 once empty. And last but not least, is the Beretta M9 sights like the other two are 3 dot fires 9 mm sighs 33.3 ounces empty."

After he named and described each firearm to me, he showed me how to hold each one and how they all worked, then I was set up with targets and was shown how to shoot, how to grip, how to adjust my stance, and how to fire each weapon. After a few hours that felt like minutes, by the end of my session with the quartermaster, we had established that guns were not my preferred weapon of choice, and we agreed that the only one I could shoot with any accuracy was the sig, so before I left him to explore the upper levels, I was issued with a sig fully loaded, three spear clips of ammo and a waist harness to carry them. "Jessica, everyone that walks around the facility is armed at all times. The nature of our work is dangerous, and you must always be prepared to defend yourself. I can see from your brief training with me you don't like guns, but I insist you carry this with you." The quartermaster gave me a stern look until I agreed, then sent me on my way. Hargreaves and I made our way to the higher levels but we skipped the mid-range weapons. When I asked why Hargreaves just said he didn't want to waste my time and it is something we can come back to if his intuition is wrong.

Shrugging this off as just something that he is more used to than others, I carried on as though I knew what to expect. I couldn't have been more wrong. As we entered the fourth floor, they greeted me with a dojo-style setup. In front of me was a beautiful woman dressed in basic gym wear, but she looked as though she had just walked off a fashion runway. "Hargreaves, you are here sooner than I expected, and you must be Jessica."

Hargreaves responded, giving me a chance to recover from being star-struck. "Hiyori, yeah, I have a feeling she might be better suited for your type of weapons, I don't think there is a point in wasting anyone's time with mid-range weapons. She is proficient enough with firearms that if something is out of reach, she can shoot it, so can you assess her and tell me what you think?"

As he finished his explanation for our early arrival, I regained my composure. "Hi, I'm guessing you are Hiyori. It's a pleasure to meet you, but can someone explain to me what's going on?"

"Yeah, sorry about that. What this idiot has neglected to say is that some people are sensitive to weapons, they get a feeling about them and are drawn to them. You see, some weapons are created using magic and anything touched with magic in its creation has something akin to a soul, something that seeks its match think of it like a destined weapon or sometimes other weapons that have been used around the paranormal community for a while can gain sentience from being used by those of power and it can cause the same affect. Not everyone can use one of these weapons, even if they are called by the weapon, it can be too powerful and can overwhelm them, but seeing as Hargreaves has brought you straight to me andhe is rarely ever wrong about these things, lets take you to the vault and see what happens."

She lead us passed the armoury, which held many weapons, most of which I could not identify. Passed various training studios that had various other personnel sparing with each other or just practicing their technique, I was lead to another set of stairs and was informed that this area was for authorised personnel only, and if I am unsuccessful in being chosen, I will not be permitted past this point again. Once up the stairs, I was lead into another armoury, the feeling in this one was different, there was an oppressive feeling about being in here, as though thousands of eyes were judging you. I had never felt so exposed, my every flaw and insecurity was being examined, but I refused to cower to this feeling. I was not the little girl that was taken to that cave and nothing was going to make me feel weak. I straightened my posture and marched into the room, I looked around and it was awe-inspiring, displayed around me was every type of traditional weapon you could imagine, and they were all so beautiful, just the sight of them could bring you to tears, there was everything from crossbows to daggers, swords and spears, and even types of weapons designed for bludgeoning your opposition. I just wanted to reach out and feel them all under my fingers, to feel the power and the connection to the objects of deadly beauty, then suddenly, my attention was pulled to the distance. In my mind, I heard two melodies playing in harmony, both desperate for my attention, but neither trying to overpower the other. At my look of uncertainty, Hiyori said, "Talk to me, Jessica, tell me what is going on. You look confused."

"It feels like I'm being called in that direction, it's hard to explain, but it's like the way Lyn would speak in my mind. It's a silent melody. What do I do?" My voice sounded desperate and in need. Hiyori indicated for Hargreaves to approach.

"Jessica, tell us what is calling you and we will bring it to you." I pointed to the display on the far wall. Hargreaves picked me up and ran to the display. I showed it was full of different types daggers. Hiyori followed and opened the case I was pointing to, and with an encouraging nod from her, I reached in and my fingers caressed a set of traditional Filipino karambits. Once both blades were in my hands, I felt a calmness as though everything was right with the world. I caressed the blades as though they were kittenscurled in my lap, and I felt as though they purred in happiness. I looked at the two instructors who had a look of shock and awe, and we sat there in comparative silence for a while just so I could adjust to this feeling of completeness.

"Jess, we should probably head to one of the training rooms to discuss what's happened and to talk about what happens now," Hargreaves said in a calm and reassuring voice. I stood as though I was on autopilot and followed him and Hiyori. I was in a state of pure bliss.

Once in one of the training rooms, Hargreaves contacted Alex, and Hiyori sat with me. Not saying a word, but watching me like a jungle cat watches her prey.

Hargreaves approached and sat with us and said, "Alex is on his way. We need to talk about the ramifications this turn of events is going to have on the training we have planned. He's also bringing Killian. Jess, are you okay? You have been silent."

"Yeah, I'm,... I don't really know. It's hard to describe. I feel calm and whole. It's like I didn't know a piece of myself was missing until it had been filled. I feel more aware, like everything is in high definition, sounds are clearer, smells are more pronounced. Why is everyone so shocked? I thought you took me there to see if a weapon would choose me?"

"We will explain everything properly when Alex gets here, but it is unusual for someone to have such a strong reaction. In that case, we are usually hard pushed to find candidates that have any pull to the weapon, so that's part of why we are so shocked," answered Hiyori.

Shortly after this revelation, Alex and Killian entered the training room both looked a little out of breath, like they had run here at top speed.

it is such good news that you have been chosen and that it happened so quickly." Jess," Alex spoke first,"

May I please look at the weapons you were drawn to?" I was still stroking my new blades and was feeling very protective of them, but Alex had done nothing to me. For me to doubt his motivations, so with slow and deliberate movements, I showed the two dagger- like blades to him. The moment I showed him the blades, his eyes widened.

"Alex, what's the matter? Did I do something wrong? Was I not supposed to touch these?" I asked. I could hear the nervous tremor in my voice, even though I was trying to project a strong front.

"No, Jessica, I am just very impressed. As far as our records show, the display case that these have been held in has only ever been used by the original warriors that held them and have never called to another. That is why we are so shocked. The fact that you have had such a strong reaction to them speaks volumes."

All the instructors were looking at each other as though something huge had happened, and I didn't understand the full ramifications of the situation. "Are you all shocked because of who the blades belonged to? Was it someone evil or dark? Should I be worried?"

Hiyori looked taken aback. "No, of course not. We would never allow something tainted in this facility, but if it makes you feel better, I will find out everything I can about the blade's origins, and I will make my findings available to you."

Her assurances made me feel a little better, and I relaxed. I noticed I could feel a calming hum coming from the blades, but only I could hear or feel it. It reminded me of kittens when they are sleeping peacefully on your lap purring as though all was right with the world.

***

Over the next few months, I find my training gets easier. Hiyori had researched my weapons that turned out to be a pair of karambits that had to be forged and wheeled by a dragon. The dragon in question had used them to protect innocents and refugees during the blood wars, and they had never called to another user since. My training with Hiyori and Hargreaves was a mix of training in the gym, hand-to-hand as well as weapons combat. To start with, we used blunt karambits, and I was taught that even a blunt weapon could be useful as they showed me how to attach pressure points and control my opponent's movements with little to no force. I was instructed to stay armed at all times with both my karambit and SIG Sauer.

While Hiyori was researching the blades, she had found out they had once been named the dragon's claws. I loved the name and chose that I would name them that as well. My sessions with Alex were progressing well. He was very patient with me, and would spend as much time on a subject as I felt I needed. He outlined rules and systems for how our society worked that I found absolutely fascinating. For example, each species and many subspecies have their own councils that govern them. Then, above them is the elder council, which is comprised of leaders from multiple supernatural groups. Then, as equals, you have the agency who enforce the rules and ensures legends stay just that. The agency works with all the groups, including humans, to ensure everyone's safety. Then above every one, you have the watcher council. I didn't really understand everything Alex said about the watchers, and he was going over materials about them, but what he says just conflicts too much for my worldview, so we agreed it was not required for my education right now, and we would pick it up at a later date. He has also taught me that every story we had been telling our children for years has been based in fact, we just didn't realise it. Everything from pixies and trolls to mermaids and unicorns, every thing I was learning was so out there that sometimes I wondered if at some point I had lost my mind and this was all just in my head. In reality, I was a mental patient that was locked away for the safety of others, then I would experience a hard session of combat training and it would bring me to my senses, or Mini would find me and know I was in dark place and would talk me out of it, she really was an amazing friend. The one real problem I was having was with the commander, he was my instructor for the more practical aspect of magic, he was a battle mage and from what he had demonstrated to me in our lessons, he was an extremely powerful one, he had spoken with the dragon breed about what abilities they should expect me to manifest and the list was long.

Killian had started easy, establishing that my strength, speed, and endurance had increased a lot more than I could have ever imagined. He said I was about as strong as a young dragon breed in human form, but after that, he wanted me to manipulate energy, or as he called it, my 'Ki'. According to him, I had a lot of it, and it should burst to come out. I honestly didn't understand what he meant. I didn't feel like I had a power, I just felt like me, but after a few weeks, he decided it was time to remove the kid gloves, and now I spent the last part of my day dodging this maniac's energy blasts, fireballs, ice spears, gusts of winds that sent me flying in any and every direction.

One afternoon, after a particularly grilling day, I wasn't in the mood to dodge his attacks, so I just walked out to the training field and sat on my ass. "What the hell do you think you're doing, Jess?"

"I'm sitting. I thought that was obvious." The look of outrage he gave me was hilarious, and if I wasn't in such a foul mood, it probably would have made me laugh.

"And how do you think you are going to dodge my assault if you are sitting, or is this telling me you can now harness your power and don't need to dodge?"

What a jackass. "Nope, I suck at this, I suck at shooting, and most of what Alex is trying to teach me is now just confusing the fuck out of me, so if you're going to attack, get on with it." I crossed my arms and glared at him. I knew I was acting like a spoilt child, but at that point, I didn't care.

"Oh, so you want a pity party, is that it?"

I sat there silently. I wouldn't give him the satisfaction of a reply.

But he didn't stop there. "What, is it too hard? Just what I thought, in the end, you are worthless. Can't hit a target at ten paces, can't protect against magic. I bet you're even failing combat training, just no one wants to tell you because they don't want to upset the poor little experiment."

"What the fuck did you just call me?" Before I knew what I was doing I was up on my feet and moving towards him. Getting ready to attack, he raised his hand, and I was flung into the air. It was like I had been hit by a gale-force wind. "What, are you scared a girl might hit you?" I screamed as I hit the dirt. "I'm scared of you, that must be a joke. I've seen toddlers with more skill than you have, the only reason you are here is that people feel sorry for you, you are useless, what would your parents think to see what a joke you've become. You must be happy they can't see you like this. I might ask Alex to forget about training you and just let the doctors run their tests. At least we might learn something then."

That was it. I snapped. I don't know how, but

electricity burst from my body and shot straight towards Killian. Power was coursing through me, but I didn't care. I would show that prick Killian that I wasn't weak or helpless. Wind whipped around me, kicking up dirt and flinging my hair around wildly. I felt my feet leave the ground. It was like I was in the storm's eye for a moment. I forgot everything around me and just felt the power. It was beautiful. Nothing else mattered. Then it stopped, and I plummeted to the ground. I landed in a heap, tangled up in my clothes.

"Jess, are you okay? Talk to me." Great, it was Killian the jackass.

"Why do you care? I'm just a useless experiment," I said. I could feel tears build. I knew that's what they all secretly thought of me. I just wasn't prepared for them to say it. I got to my feet and made a quick retreat to my room. I couldn't stand to have anyone else look at me with pity today.

Chapter 5

The next few days, I locked myself away, surveying what I had in my mini fridge. I couldn't bring myself to go back out there and see the people I had trusted and thought of as friends, not knowing that they just think of me like some lost, useless puppy at best and worst, a failed experiment that needed to be put down. It didn't help that since the incident with Killian, anytime I got upset, electrical energy would arch over my body and between my fingers until I calmed down again. Whatever had happened had broken me, and all I could think is there are going to lock me up and not let me out because I'm too dangerous.

Knock, knock, knock.

"Jess, it's me," came Mini's voice from beyond the door. "Look, we all know what happened, so we've been trying to give you space, but I'm getting worried about you. I can feel your emotions. Remember, it's not good to be alone when you're feeling like this. Come on, let me in. I've brought food, you must get sick of mini fridge snacks." I got up and made my way to the door. Once I let her in, I retreated to my bed and curled into my blanket.

"Here you go hun, eat this. It will make you feel a little better," she said as she set a large tray of food next to me. Next, she pulled out a few bottles of water.

"So do you want to tell me about it?" she asked, keeping her tone calm.

"I assumed you already know what happened. That's why you're here, isn't it?" I asked between mouthfuls of food. She was right—I really needed the food.

"I know what Killian told everyone, but I would really like to hear your side."

I spent some time going over how my day had gone and then told her about what had happened with Killian and all the things he said to me. As I told her, I could see she was getting irritated and thought it was because of me. "I'm sorry, I should have known the only reason Alex wanted me here was because of the things Jeremiah did to me. he wants to make sure I'm not a threat, I see that now." As I spoke, electric crackled over my body. *Shit, I need to calm down. I need to breathe.*

Once I calmed down, Mini smiled at me. "First thing's first." She held up her hand and lifted a finger. "I am not angry at you. I am, however, extremely pissed at Killian, and he will incur my wrath at a later date." As she finished, she lifted another finger. "What he said wasn't true, no one, including him, feels like that about you."

I objected, but she spoke over me. "Jess, he saw you had a rough day and he thought he would play on your insecurities to see if he could get you to unleash some of your power. Now, we can agree that you definitely had a showing of power, but the way he went about it was wrong. I can assure you that he regrets doing it and I am going to make him suffer for it."

I nodded as she finished speaking. "I'm sorry I made you worry," I said, then sobbed. "You really don't hate me, right?" I asked.

"I promise less none of us to hate you, but Killian might hate me once I'm finished with him."

"Please don't punish him. He was only trying to help, I guess."

"I will think about it, but I'm not making any promises. I'm not as forgiving as you. Now, finish eating, then you can get some rest before training begins again tomorrow."

***

I did as I was told, and Mini left my room so I could rest. The next day, my training restarted. All of my instructors greeted me warmly and said they had heard about what had happened and assured me that none of them felt negatively towards me. Even Killian apologised, although I noticed him walking with a limp. No one would tell me what happened to him. The only thing they would say is he slipped, then smile and change the subject. I had a feeling Mini was responsible for his accident.

After a few more months of training, I was finally feeling like I was doing well. Alex still confused me when it came to the paranormal world, but I had a feeling that I would only really start to understand it by living in it. I was more proficient with my sig, but I would never be a sharp shooter. The best I could say is that I can hit the target I'm aiming for eight times out of ten, but it was a marked improvement from when I had started. My training with my karambi's and general hand-to-hand is where I excelled. I hadn't been able to win against Hioryi or Hargreaves yet, but I was lasting a good few minutes before they pulled me to the mat. Even my time with Killian was more productive than it used to be, although I swear he enjoys making me miserable. Still, every day I endure it, hoping that today will be the day that I can wipe the grin from his face. In my defence, now I don't just dodge his attacks, I now have enough control to swat some of his blasts off course, but those wind attacks always kick my ass. Sometimes, when I'm focusing my energy to swat a blast out of my way, I think I can see the faint outline of iridescent scales on my skin, but when I try to get a closer look they are gone, then I realise it must just be the light hitting my sweat-covered body a certain way or my mind playing tricks on me.

***

It felt like I had just closed my eyes when the banging started coming from my door. Refusing to pay any attention to it, I rolled over and covered my head with my pillow, just praying for whoever it was to just go away. But no, the banging intensified until Mini screamed from the top of her lungs, "Jess I know you're in there. Now wake up, and open the door or I'm not taking you with me...."

What the hell? She couldn't mean she was taking me on a mission. I had been begging for weeks to be assigned a real case. I threw the duvet off and jumped from my bed and pulled my apartment door open. Standing in front of me was a very serious-looking Minerva. "Well, get dressed and meet me at Alex's office. And do me a favour, and try not to look too excited."

I can't believe I was getting to go on a mission with Mini. Sure, I have been able to shadow a few of the senior instructors, but maybe this time I will get in on the action. I ran to my bathroom, got a quick shower and made myself presentable. For me, that ended up with me dressed in loose jeans, a t-shirt, and a fitted jacket that would conceal my gun and knife rig. As per my instructor's demands, I didn't go anywhere without my weapons. If I didn't have them with me, I somehow felt naked and vulnerable. Once ready, I ran to Alex's office.

Outside his door, I took a steadying breath to get my nerves and excitement under control. After a few seconds feeling I was ready for whatever was to come next, I entered the office. Everyone wore a grim expression.

"Jessica," Alex announced while motioning me towards his desk. "Please, take a seat, and I will explain your assignment. I would like you to join Minerva in a case in London. Now, I know you have shadowed a few of the instructors regarding the work we do, but this will not be like that. You are going to be working this case like any other agent would, so I would like you to accept this new identification." Alex handed me a leather wallet. Inside, it contained a badge, along with a plastic identification card. I was shocked and wasn't expecting this. "Thank you, but are you sure I am ready?"

"Your instructors seem to think you are ready, and I agree, although when not actively on a case, I still expect you to train. Commander Killian has also stated that you still need a lot of work on your dragon gifts, but the control you have now should be sufficient."

For a moment, it stunned me. I knew I had been working my butt off, but I didn't realise that my instructors thought this highly of me.

"Thank you, I will try to make you all proud that you have taken a chance on me."

"I'm sure you will do your best, and I'm going to be partnering you with Mini."

I gave my friend a quick look of apprehension, worried that she might think I was a burden, but she just gave me a beaming smile and focused back on what Alex was saying.

"As I was saying, this case isn't ideal as a first, but it's also best to get it out of the way. You will head to London. We have had a report of a series of unsolved murders which have been concerning us, and I've just got off the phone. when I sent for you, another victim has been discovered. you will head straight to the crime scene and are to take over the investigation."

"Where in London?" I asked.

"Chelsea Park Gardens. You will be met at the site by one of our crime techs, and everything has been cordoned off. You will be stationed at one of our field offices and they have been notified to expect you. I've put together a briefing pack, and I expect you both to read it thoroughly before you arrive. You will have a direct flight to London Stansted, and a driver waiting to take you both to Chelsea Park Gardens. I have faith that you will both do us proud but if you run into difficulties just ask for help." He handed us our briefing packs and dismissed us.

Chapter 6

Mini and I rushed to our rooms and packed a bag of essentials, briefing file in hand. I ran to the car that would take us to the plane. Sitting next to Mini, I could see that she was tense.

"Do you want to talk about what's on your mind?" I asked, trying to respect her boundaries. Over the last few months, I had discovered that Mini could sometimes get overwhelmed by her empathic abilities and would block herself from using it unless she had so. But if emotions around her ran too high, or if people touched her without her being prepared, she would get the raw source of all the emotions around her and the way she explained it, I could cause her physical pain.

"Yeah, I'm okay hun. I just took a glance at the file and I think you may have to do a lot of the heavy lifting in this case."

"I don't understand, Mini. You have done this before. I thought I would only assist." Fear and self-doubt ate away at me as the thought of me taking lead sunk in.

"Jess, I have faith in you, and so does everyone else. Otherwise, they wouldn't be putting you in the field, but to explain, anywhere that has experienced any significant exposure to emotions will hold an echo of that emotion. As someone with an empathic gift, I can pick up on those echoes. And although those echoes diminish with time, with this being so fresh, it might be too much and I might miss something, so I might not always be able to control the emotions I'm feeling."

"Okay, I understand and will do what I can to help."

"Thank you, Jess, now I think it's time we delve into these briefings." She smiled at me, but I could tell it was strained she was trying to put on a brave face."

***

We arrived at the crime scene, and after reading the file Alex had given us, I could understand why Mini looked so terrified. "If you want to stay out here I'm sure I can take care of everything inside." She looked dry, as though getting any closer would make her physically sick.

"Thanks for the offer, but I should be okay."

Our drive exited the car and opened the door for us. "I will look after your ba's here and wait for your return," he said matter-of-factly then got back into the car. I looked at him as though he had just slapped me in the face with a wet fish. I wasn't sure if this was correct behaviour for a driver, but it definitely took me by surprise. The look on my face must have said as much because Mini broke down laughing. "Oh, I'm sorry, but the look or your face in our current situation was just so surreal." She took a moment to compose herself then we headed towards the police cordon.

The closer we got to the cordon, the worse Mini looked, but I would respect her decision and wouldn't mention anything more about it. But even I could feel the tension, it was like a foul taste left at the back of my mouth. A uniformed officer attempted to stop us from crossing under the police tape.

"I'm sorry, ladies, this is a secure crime scene. I can't allow you to pass." Before I could say a word, Mini seeped in front of the officer ."I'm sorry, officer, but could you direct us to the person in charge, our presence was requested and we should be expected."

"Oh, I'm sorry ma'am, I wasn't informed. If you would like to follow me."

Mini gave me a knowing look. The sneaky shit had pushed him with her power. Well, at least it sped things up a bit. He took us towards the house and my nose was assaulted with the smell that hit me. It was a rancid mixture of fear, blood, despair, and pain. It was like approaching an abandoned slaughterhouse. I tried to hold my nose and breathe through my mouth, but that was just as bad. Even the uniformed officer was covering his nose. As we entered the front door, the first thing I noticed was the silence. All of my instructors and even my experience shadowing others had always shown me that crime scenes are noisy, usually, chatter and theories are flying around. But it was so quiet you could hear a pin drop. Everyone was processing the scene in silence. The scene itself is the worse than I had imagined. Looking over to Mini, I could tell it was worse than she was expecting and with her being an empath, she must have been picking up on everyone's reactions and the last moments of the victim's pain and terror, do you need to wait outside? I know this" Mini," I asked in a hushed tone that I knew she could hear,"

t easy for you."'isn"Jess, I will be fine. I'm shielding myself now. I just wasn't expecting that wave of emotions. It was intense and not in a good way."

"Okay, let's get this over with."

Mini continued to follow the uniformed officer, but I started looking around the crime scene. After coming through the small entrance hall, they went up a staircase on the right to the first floor, but I went left into what appeared to be a reception room. This was obviously where the attack started. Crime techs worked quickly around me, taking pictures of blood spatter, cataloguing everything in the room so we could recreate it later. I took a deep calming breath as I was taught to. I pictured myself in a copy of the room, but it was empty, and unleashed my other senses trying to piece together what went down in this beautiful picture of suburban bliss. I sorted the smells and feelings that I could pick up, disregarding the ones that were more recent, focusing on the older, fainter signs. Focusing on the room again, I could make out a basic pattern of how this had started. A woman went to the door and let in two strangers. On the way back to the reception room, I could pick up on a nervousness. Who ever these visitors were, they made her uncomfortable. Once they made it to the centre of the room, three others entered. From what I could see was a dining room, the visitors had interrupted dinner. I could smell a man and two children. A boy and a girl come to the reception room like they had been called in, intermingled with these smells and feelings I got a surge of fear so strong it must have near driven them mad. I circled the room, taking in more of the surroundings and trying to piece together what had happened. The man and children didn't seem to move from where they stood for a while, like they had been frozen in place. The two visitors stood close to the woman, where they would have been standing was a puddle of blood on the carpet and cast off spray on the walls and ceiling. If I had to guess, I would say whatever they did, they did it as a statement to ensure the other's compliance. From the pool of blood I noticed droplets leading to the stairs. The remaining scent trails of all five individuals seemed to lead in the same direction. I had a choice: I could either follow the blood down or head up and find Mini. My curiosity got the better of me, and I followed the blood and scent trail.

The further down I went, the stronger the smell of blood and fear. No, not fear, it was more like terror. As I reached the bottom of the staircase I walked into what appeared to be an entertaining area, but it was in complete disarray. Furniture was thrown everywhere and the blood spatter on the walls, ceiling, and floor was horrendous. To the left of me, a set of double doors lay discarded. Beyond them was a home office that lay ransacked. It appeared our guests had been looking for something. I tried to refocus again, attempting to arrange the information my senses were giving me, but everything was confusing. The scent trails all intermingled, and with so much blood, it was hard to concentrate. The main bodies had been removed but there were still bits of discarded flesh strewn everywhere. I was really not looking forward to seeing the medical examiner. I approached one of the forensic technicians and asked how bad the bodies were and if he could give me a rough idea on where they were left in the room. He looked shocked that I was talking to him and spoke with a slight stutter.

"The female's body is nearly unrecognisable. The only way you can tell it was a human body was the skeletal structure." My stomach was close to emptying its contents, but I held it back. "The boy was nearly as bad. They left his body by the home office. The male looked like he had be tortured, his finger and toenails had been torn out, the bones in his fingers and hands had been broken, all his joints appeared to be dislocated, and it also looked like they pulled several of his teeth out." The forensic tech was turning paler with every word, and once he was done with his explanation, he left the room. I could only assume that it was to find a safe place to vomit, because if I hadn't just realised something, I would have been joining him. Only three bodies had been discovered. We had a witness.

I raced back up the stairs. My goal was to find Mini and get a search started. As I got to the next floor, I heard Mini's voice coming from the reception room that I had been in a little while ago. I stepped into the room to find her in a standoff with a plain-clothed officer, he had a look about him that screamed arrogant ass. "Look, little girl, I didn't request your help and I don't need your help. Now, get the hell out of my crime scene." Mini puffed up like a blowfish. This guy was getting to her. "Check your over-inflated ego at the fucking door. They have requested us to be here, you obviously can't solve the homicides." I heard a snigger next to me. "Damn, she's on fire. Look at him. He's been struck dumb."

"And who might you be, I ask?"

"Sorry, I should have introduced myself earlier. I'm Keith. The London office sent me to help you guys settle in. I'm usually a lab monkey, but it seems to be all hands on deck for this before it gets much more publicity."

m Jess and we need to break this up. I have information that I believe is relevant and'Okay, Keith, I"t know better, it looked as'urgent." We looked at each other and then at the pair in front of us. If I didn though the argument was rapidly going to turn into a fistfight. Keith and I grumbled in unison and waded towards the argument. I took a deep breath, and channelling as much authority into my voice as I could, I

Enough!"" bellowed, The sound of my voice was so loud it seemed to shake the windows. Everyone stopped what they were doing and just looked at me. If I had to guess, I think I scared the life out of a few of them. I even scared myself. I looked at Mini and Keith, both of who were hiding giant grins and suppressing a giggle. I took charge while everyone else was still in a state of shock. "Now that the pair of you have shut up, I have a question. How many bodies have been found?" They all looked at me like I had grown a third head. "Do I seriously have to ask again?" The officer who had been arguing with Mini turned to me.

"And who the fuck might you be, little miss loudmouth?"

"You can call me Jessica. I'm Minerva's partner on this assignment. I'm assuming you have a name, or should I just address you as assclown?" The shocked expression on his face was priceless, but it was soon replaced with a scowl. "I'm DCI Duncan Lancaster, as I was explaining to your associate, we don't need your help." I stopped him right there.

"Look, I'm not in the mood for a pissing contest. Just tell me, have you found the witness?"

"What the fuck are you talking about? There was no witness. We got an anonymous call like all the others."

"How many bodies did you find?" I asked.

"Three, why, what's so important about that? They were all found downstairs. If you want the cause of death, ask your friend over there. He's already sent them for autopsy at your facility."

I took a breath, trying to control my anger, but something in me snapped. "Look around you cock womble. How many people live in this house? How many dinner plates have been left at the table, and how many bedrooms? Fuck me, it doesn't take a genius to see that two children lived here and two fucking adults. I'm assuming the parents. Where the fuck is the girl if you haven't found a body?" I let my statement sit in the air. All eyes focused on me, I took another calming breath. "Why are you looking at me? Find the girl. I have a feeling she's still in the house somewhere." After I spoke, the house became a hive of activity.

Chapter 7

As everyone began rushing around the house looking in all the obvious places, I took Mini and Keith downstairs to the entertainment area. "I don't know why, but I'm positive she's down here," I explained as we made our way down. "Mini, I know it's going to be intense, but I need you to see if you can pickup on her emotions." I knew I was asking a lot, she was already struggling in the rest of the house, it was going to be a hell of a lot worse for her down here.

"I will manage. We need to find this kid. I can't even imagine what she's already been through." It didn't take us long to find her hiding in a secure wine cellar.

I have no clue how she got away, but getting into the wine cellar must have been too much for the two attackers. I would need to check if it was re-enforced.

Mini crouched near the entrance. "Hey there, my

name is Mini. I'm here to help. Can you open the door a little for me sweetheart?" Her tone was calming, and I could tell she was weaving magic into her words trying to get the girl to lower her guard and to trust us."

"Where is she?" DCI Lancaster demanded as he came into the room. "Keep your voice down, my partner is trying to get her to come out and the safer she feels the easier that will be," I said stepping into his path. "Get out of my way." Unfortunately, he managed to get around me just as Mini had convinced our witness to open the door just a fraction to prove that we would not be going to hurt her.

Seeing the little girl huddle away from the door like an injured animal, silent tears pouring down her cheeks, shaking like a leaf but with an iron grip on a knife broke my heart, and I lost track of what Lancaster was doing. He forced his way forward, pushing Mini out of the way and startling the girl. *Big mistake.* The girl slashed and stabbed with all her might. She scored a brilliant hit to the detective's arm. I let out a giggle and was awarded a death glare from the detective. "Well, what did you expect? The kid is scared, get out of the way and let us handle this."

Mini edged closer. Keith and I worked to keep everyone else at a distance. I felt the slight surge of power emit from my partner as she spoke to the girl. "Sorry about that jerk. He was in the wrong, he shouldn't have tried to force his way in." The girl studied Mini, her eyes glazing over slightly as though she was entering a daze. "Now, me and my friend are here to help you, sweetheart. Can you let us do that?" As she kept talking, the more power she was feeding into her words, the girl nodded her head. Everything about her relaxed. I expected her grip on the weapon to slip, but it was still as firm as when we began. I moved towards Mini and spoke as softly as I could. "Whatever you do, don't take the knife away." She nodded. She understood.

I made my way over to Lancaster to see how badly he was injured. "Well, that was eventful. Do you need stitches, or are you going to be okay with just some antiseptic and a dressing?" He answered with a sneer. "Well, seeing that civility seems to be beyond you right now, let's just get to the point." This seemed to shock him. "I'm here to do a job. We didn't mean to piss in cornflakes, but sometimes, that happens. Your boss requested our help. To be able to help, I need information. You have that information." I gave him a second to let that sink in.

"I'm sorry, it's just a very stressful case, and having you guys come in and take it is frustrating."

"I get that, but we aren't taking you out of the case. Yes, we will follow our own leads, but that doesn't mean you can't follow yours, all I'm asking for is an exchange of information, so we can stop any more scenes like these? What can you tell me about the case, and I don't mean what I can read in the file."

He gave me a look as though he was only just seeing me for the first time. "You mean you want my help? Usually, when other agencies get involved, they want all the credit."

"I don't care about credit. You can tell everyone that you solved the case for all I care. I will even write my report to make you look like a hero if that's what you want. I just need your input so we can stop this psycho."

He looked surprised at my request for information. "You… you want my input?"

"Yes, now can you tell me are there any similarities with the other cases? You were the lead on this from the first case, so what are your impressions? Leave nothing out, even if you think it's impossible or sounds crazy."

"What good will that do? You have my file. I included all my notes. I don't think I left anything out." I began pacing back and forth, trying to use some of my nervous energy.

"I've read your notes, but it's human nature to skim over things that don't make sense. I'm asking you, so tell me what you're thinking. What are your theories?"

"I can't cover everything here. I need to go through my notes and organise my thoughts, but I would be happy to share my notes, findings, and theories with your team."

"Do you think this is connected to the other cases?

Could it be a copycat?"

"I think they are all connected. We have kept most of these out of the media, but we have had homeless people going missing for weeks and months then showing up dead. Child abduction cases have skyrocketed in the last 18 months, with a lot of the missing showing up dead with the cause of death being put down to substance abuse. Drug dealers are turning up in the same state as this family. As I said, most of this has been unreported, and I'm only being able to connect it all after a lot of digging." He stopped to take a breath.

This guy has connected the same dots as Alexander. "Okay, we need to finish up here. The kid will come with my team, and I'm assuming all evidence from all related cases is being sent to our facility." At my question, he just nodded an affirmative. "I would also like you to bring your case notes to the office tomorrow. It will give us time to develop a working theory of what is going on. Is noon enough time for you to get everything together?" He gave me another nod.

"Okay then. I need to assemble my team and the witness, then head to our field office. If you discover anything else, brief us tomorrow, but if it's urgent and you feel it can't wait, call me immediately." I handed him my card, hoping he would call us if he got any leads. The last thing we needed was a detective going missing. I made my way back to Keith and Mini, and was shocked to find that they had managed to get the girl out of hiding. Although she was still shielding her self away behind them both, and I could still see the knife clutched tightly in her small hands.

"Okay, I've left things in the detective's hands and arranged a debrief with him for noon tomorrow at the office." They both nodded, and Mini interrupted me before I could say anything else. "Jess, this is Alisha. I've explained that we are her friends and we are going to take her somewhere safe." As she was talking to me, Alisha poked her head out and gave me a tentative look up and down. She whispered something to her human shields, and I could tell it had tickled Mini.

"Oh, Alisha, I promise you wholeheartedly that she is very nice and not nearly as mean as she looks. I'll tell you a secret, she has a weakness for cupcakes and cookies all you need to do is give her a cake and she becomes as cute and adorable as a newborn kitten."

My jaw hit the floor. First of all, I am not that bad, I just enjoy a good pastry cake or cookie. Tell me anyone who doesn't, and second, am I really that scary looking? Thinking back to how I used to be described before, I lost everything people always said was cute, but I guess all the training and exercise had changed me more than I realised. Alisha peeked at me again, this time with a huge grin. I knelt down, bringing myself to eye level with her.

"Well, since Mini seems to have a problem with sweet treats, it means there will be more for you and me." Alisha let out a slight giggle, and we lead her back to the car. Walking through the house, we told her to keep her eyes on the floor and we did our best to block her view of the carnage around us. We couldn't block everything, but we did our best to block the worst. My heart broke as she started to cry silently, if I could hold her and cry I would, but my tears would do nothing for her, and I couldn't indulge in my sorrow, not now, not when her and others like her depended on my strength. I need to be strong forthis child. As we got Alisha settle in the back of the car so Keith and Mini could be on either side of her like two imposing sentinels, I confirmed arrangements with DCI Lancaster and we made our way towards the field office. Within minutes of the drive starting, I heard a quiet series of snores coming from behind me. I looked around to find Alisha passed out with her head propped on Mini's shoulder. At my questioning look, she shrugged. "The poor thing was exhausted, so I just gave her a gentle emotional nudge to get her to sleep, but she still won't let go of that bloody knife." I wasn't surprised, the rest of the journey was completed in relative silence. I think we where all just try to process the horror that we had seen.

***

Arriving at the London field office was a surprise. I expected it to be located in a section of a police station or something, but this was a modern office building. If I didn't know better, I would say it was a high-end corporate building, not a field office for the paranormal defence agency.our driver opened the door and said"I will take care of your luggage for you, the medical team is on standby to examine the child and ensure she is in good health and I was informed that a conference room has been set up for your use. All these details have been emailed to Keith, and I've been instructed to let you know he will be your liaison for the remainder of your visit."

Before I could comment or thank him, he was out the door and making his way to the back to hold the door for Mini. Instead of waking Alisha, we carried her. Our first port of call was going to be the medical wing. We followed Keith as he checked us in with security and headed to the third floor where we found a top of the line medical facility. We lay Alisha on one of the vacant beds and spoke to one of the nurses to ensure that she would be okay. Mini insisted on staying with Alisha so she would have a familiar face when she woke up, and she could use her empathic abilities to calm her down if necessary.

"Jess, I know the original plan was for this to be a team assignment, but I can't leave her like this, it's not right, so I need you to handle it as best you can. Just keep me in the loop, I will try to get as much information out of Alisha, and I will run things here and coordinate everything as needed." Seeing the way Mini was with Alisha, I couldn't say I was surprised by her choice.

"That's fine, but promise me that if the shit hits the fan, you will join my in the field to deal with it."

"Of course I will, hun, but I don't think you'll need me. I have faith in you." Taking that as my dismissal from the ward, I went to leave, expecting Keith to be in my wake, but he held up a hand showing for me to stop.

"If you are planning on staying here with Alisha, I will get a workstation set up in here for you so you can work the case and video conference the briefing room, and it will save us constantly relaying messages. I will also see if we can set you up with a comms link so Jess can stay in contact with you while in the field."

"Wow, that would be great, Keith. What do you think, Mini? Will that setup works for you?"

"Sounds great to me. At least that way, I can still give input and support as you need it."

As she said, this Keith was straight on the phone making the arrangements. I lent over, hoping I was out of Keith's earshot. "Mini, are you sure I can do this? I thought I would be following your lead. What if I make mistakes and more people die? What if I can't stop whoever is doing this? I've only read about investigations and watched others doing them. Are you sure I'm ready?"

"Jess, I wouldn't have accepted you as my partner if I didn't think you could handle yourself. You finished the agency's training quicker than any recruit before you, all the instructors are amazed by your progress. At the crime scene you found a witness, and I'm sure you have had other insights that you will reveal as we investigate further, don't doubt yourself."

What Mini had said caused me to develop a lump in my throat and I couldn't express the way I felt, but she just nodded and said, "I understand Jess, and I love you. Now, go get organised then get some rest. I get a feeling we won't be getting much more of it anytime soon."

With me being dismissed by Mini, I grabbed Keith and asked him to take me to the briefing room we would be using.

"Yeah, come with me. You'll be on the fifth floor, it's also where we keep the armoury. The briefing room is next to the facility chief's office, so I'm sure we will be seeing him over the day." He led us to an elevator and pushed the button for the fifth floor. "So, you're going to be the lead investigator on this."

I took a nervous gulp at his question. "Yep, it looks like it's down to me to keep everything on track."

"I have complete faith in you, Jessica, and the entire agency has your back, so if you need anything, you just need to ask."

"Thank you, it means a lot."

"And I'm going to stick with you guys on the case, so you won't be alone."

I gave him a grateful smile as he showed me into the briefing room. They had already set up the existing case files and whiteboards for us to work on. They had also developed a timeline for the case that we knew about. As I looked this over, I realised everything I assumed I would need to do tonight had alreadybeen done.

I looked at Keith, giving him an inquisitive look. "We were told that you had a long journey, and with everything you've experienced today, I thought I would get everything set up so now you can get a few hours rest before DCI Lancaster arrives with his notes and case files. I have also instructed the nurse to ensure Mini gets some rest. Would you like me to take you to your dorm room?"

"That would be great, but I thought we would stay at a hotel?"

"The top few floors have been turned into living quarters for people that have a tendency to work too much, or if we have visitors from other facilities." He took me to my quarters in relative silence. Once we got there, he handed me a key card and said he would wake me at 7 a.m. so we would have five hours to sort things before the detective arrives with his insights. I was also informed that the room had a fully stocked and functioning kitchen.

"Thank you, but I will probably just try to get some sleep, it's been a long day/"He left me to my thoughts as

I closed the door.

***

A fresh day and a fresh start. I checked on Mini and Alisha when I was on my way to the briefing room. Alisha was sleeping, but Mini was up and already logged in to her very impressive tech set up. She informed me she was ready to go, and I needed to go to the briefing room so she could catch me up on what she had found so far.

Being in the briefing room was a little overwhelming, but I had to push on. The tech crew that Keith had mentioned had set up multiple display screens and cameras. Mini's voice sounded from one screen, startling me and making me squeal. "Stop being impressed and let's get on with some work." She giggled a little at my reaction. "That was so not funny, Mini, you nearly gave me a heart attack."

"Please, it will take more than a little fright to kill you off."

"Okay, so what have you discovered so far?"

"We have a huge problem. From the information here and a quick database search on missing persons and homicides that have hit a brick wall, I think this has been going on for at least 18 months, possibly 24, and the bodies that I have linked to this case are getting progressively worse. The first few bodies had been killed in violent ways but nothing like the bodies from last night."

Keith entered the conference room while Mini was telling me what she had found. "Well, I have the lab techs working on the physical evidence right now so they should be able to get some sort of trace evidence that may give us some leads as to what type of monster we are dealing with."

I gave him an appraising look. "Do you have any insights you would like to share with us?"

The only thing we know for sure is that these aren't all the victims. These are just the humans, we have been hearing for a while that this is happening in the paranormal community too, but no one is willing to come forward and admit that they are losing those in their care." I gave him a look of confusion. "Are you telling me that this is happening in the paranormal community and we don't know about it? How is that possible?" I asked.

Mini's voice came across the speakers. "Jess, Alex has told you about this before, remember? The agencies can only deal with things that are reported, but usually the individual leaders for the community will deal with the problems. They have their own enforcers and although they acknowledge our authority, they hate appearing weak by relying on us." I could remember the lesson she was talking about. It was one of the many I had difficulty wrapping my head around. I let out a sigh of frustration and held up my hands in surender. "Okay, I get it, but how do we find out if this is as big a problem as we believe?"

Keith held up his hand to get our attention. "We aren't in the classroom, Keith. If you have a suggestion, just throw it out there."

He gave me a nervous smile and said, "So figuring that this might end up being a problem, I may have arranged a few meetings with the various representatives for the paranormal factions in the area after you met with DCI Lancaster."

"Okay, that's good news. Hopefully we will be able to get some help, or at the very least some information from them." Mini and Keith didn't seem to hold the same opinion, but didn't voice their doubt. "So, who have you set up appointments with and are they coming here?" I asked, my voice full of hope.

"I have a meeting booked with the mages. You have two meetings booked, one with the vampire council and the other with the dragon's court. They have insisted that they will only meet with you and no one else from the agency can accompany you."

"Did they say why it's so important that I go alone?"

"No, but please be careful. Those two factions are too powerful, and they have too much influence for their own good. I have a feeling it's some sort of test. Just please try not to offend them."

Great, dealing with two of the power players of London was not on my to-do list, but if they are going out of their way to meet me, they are scared, or they could be a part of this. *Well, there's only going to be one way to get the answers I want and that's to meet them.*

"Who's meeting with the shifters? They must have a ruling alpha that is willing to talk to us?" "Unfortunately, they are refusing to cooperate at this current time. They haven't given a reason, but they seem to be hiding something. I just can't figure out what. If I get any updates, you will be the first toknow."

***

The meeting with DCI Lancaster went about as well as I expected. He had the names and descriptions of dozens of missing persons. None had officially been reported because they were vagrants and those that lived a transient lifestyle. He also had an impressive list of suspicious deaths that had been attributed to drug overdoses or heart attacks and other vague reasons. Through a quick rundown of what he had, I could see he was definitely on to something, but no one but him had bothered to try and connect the dots. After assuring him that I would keep the lines of communication open with him and that if he had any leads that he could reach me any time, night or day, I saw him out of the building and got ready for my meeting with the vampire council.

Chapter 8

Driving up to the vampire council's estate always freaked me out. The place was huge. I didn't see anyone about the grounds, but I knew I was being watched. The gate opened without me needing to stop, and I carried on up the winding driveway until I stopped in front of the large double doors. I took one last fortifying breath before I exited my car and walked up the steps. As I reached the door, it opened, and I faced the fake smile of someone recently turned. This vampire couldn't have been more than a few months old. He still had the telltale sign of red eyes that all blood suckers have when the blood lust was in control of their actions. Older vamps can control this so they can appear less threatening to humans. "You must be Jessica from the agency. My masters are waiting for you in the library. Please follow me." Without another word, he turned and walked away, leading me to my destination. They were sticklers for protocol, so I let him do his job without causing trouble, as we approached the library, I could feel the pulse of power radiating from the room it looks like they have more than a few elders in attendance for our little conversation, this should be fun…

Entering a room full of vampires is never something to look forward to doing. Well, time to put on my big girl panties and get this shit done. I walked into the library like I owned the place, making note of where everyone was. It seemed to a casual observer that they were mostly scattered throughout the room, engrossed in their own pleasures. Some reading books, others smoking cigars, and a few even gathered into small groups and having conversations, but the moment my chaperone left, closing the door behind me, they all turned and focused solely on me. The gaze alone was bad enough, but the intensity of the power and blood lust coming from them nearly brought me to my knees. I just had to breathe and not react, if I lashed out with my power, this would end badly, so I just had to wait until they were satisfied that I wasn't some sort of loose cannon. Minutes passed, and then I felt the wave of power lessen it felt like I was stood there for hours trying to resist the urge to let loose. Once I got my rage under control, they all turned back to their earlier pursuits, all but one, anyway. This one walked towards me and gestured for me to take a seat at a small coffee table. The gentleman reached for my hand to introduce himself, but I pulled my hand away and explained that I don't like to be touched. He inclined his head ina sign that he understood, then said, "Am I correct In my assumption that you are Jessica, from the agency?" I reply with a quick yes. "Am I also correct in my information that you are one of the dragon blood?" As he asked this, his eyes narrowed in a calculating way. I hate vampires.

"Yes, you are right, I am one of the dragon's blood, but that is not why I am here. As you know, there hasbeen an incident, and the agency has been called in to investigate as it seems to be supernatural in origin. You should be aware of this because you are all here to put on this little demonstration of power. Now cut the crap and lets get on with this meeting." As I said this, a ghost of a smile graced his face. "You are as straightforward as your reputation says. Well, it's like you said. We have been appraised of the situation, but as it stands, we can't see why it concerns any from the vampire community." At this I was shocked. They couldn't be that stupid, could they?

"Are you seriously asking me why this concerns you? You are the ones that requested my attendance at this meeting. Firstly, a family was skinned alive. Whoever or whatever did it was powerful enough to hold them in some sort of thrall or trance while they did it. Secondly, we suspect who ever is responsible is connected to a series of mysterious deaths and reports of missing persons going back at least 18 months, and you can't think of any reason that I came here? There are dozens if not more vampire subspecies that fit the base profile. Now, we don't know for sure that it is one of these, but I would have assumed that you wanted to help us apprehend those responsible. Am I making it clear now why it is a concern for the vampire council?"

"I think its time for you to leave. Let me show you the way."

"Don't bother. I will find my way out. Thanks for nothing." As I left the library, all the remaining council members converged on the one I was speaking to. I'm sure they know more than they are letting on. Starting up my car, I looked out onto the road ahead. I thought if this is how the vampires had reacted, may the gods protect me, because I had a feeling the dragons would be worse. I put my car in gear and was about to drive off when there was a sudden knock at my door that startled me. Winding down my window, I was greeted with an annoyingly cheerful grin followed by a very gentle and delicate voice, the type of voice that would be classed as angelic and beautiful, saying, "My name is Abigail, and it is a pleasure to meet you, Jessica. I assume your meeting with the council didn't go as well as you had hoped?"

I sighed and answered this strange little critter. "Yes, the meeting wasn't as productive as I would have hoped, but it was what I was expecting." While answering these questions, I was slowly grasping my firearm, ready to defend myself. The girl calling herself Abigail looked straight to my arm and smiled. "Now, Jessica, that's no way to treat someone who only wants to help. Let me come to your meeting with the dragon representative. I'm sure they will answer more fully and honesty with me there, and I can always help provide a little extra muscle to your team. I will even say please."

I didn't know why but my instincts were telling me that Abigail was on the level and wouldn't do anything to deliberately put me in danger. "Fine, get in, but try any funny business and I will kill you." I put as much steel into my voice as humanly possible, but still, she just giggled to herself as though I just said the funniest thing she had ever heard. She got in and buckled up before I drove out.

***

The dragon breed, like many in the supernatural community, could blend in with humans, and except for the truly ancient ones, they aren't as large as people think. The biggest I had ever seen was Lyn, but from what I've been told, they can get as big as a mountain. On average they are about the size of one or two double decker buses, but they rarely use the dragon form on this plane of existence. When they are required to mingle with the lesser being, they will transform into a human form. Many of the ones that interact with humans regularly are in charge of big businesses, or control those in power in different countries. The legends and stories are true for the most part when they say they dragons are only concerned in their self-interest.

My sat-nav pinged to alert me that we had reached the destination that I had been given, and it took me a moment to process what I was seeing. This had to have been a joke— they had arranged to meet me at an old style pub called 'The Dragon's Keep'. I couldn't keep a straight face. Who knew that dragons had a sense of humour?

Abigail got out of the car, and I met her at the entrance of the pub. As we entered we were greeted by a very dishevelled waitress who asked if it was just a party of two. Before we had a chance to respond, a very tall, very handsome man interrupted, "It's okay, Mona, these lovely ladies will be joining me in the corner booth."

"Gudmundur, I didn't see you there. I will see your guests to your usual table, sir. This way, please, ladies." The waitress was off at top speed, signalling for us to follow her. She sat us at a corner table with a wrap around couch. The seating arrangement that had a clear view of the entire venue, and I could see all exits and escape routes. This dragon was tipping his hand a little, showing us all the vulnerabilities that could be exploited if this conversation turned nasty, which was often the case when it came to the dragon breed.

Gudmundur sat next to Abigail, and I got the impression they knew each other. You never saw vampires and dragons acting so friendly towards each other, but these two seemed to be like old friends, enjoying breakfast at their local greasy spoons. "Okay you two, spill what the fuck is going on. I have been called to a brutal murder case, I have a little girl stashed at the agency, my boss has asked for the representatives from the supernatural councils to come together and help, but so far, I have been snubbed by the vamps, had the blood-sucking version of the energiser bunny decide to tag along with me with zero explanation as to why, then we come here as requested to meet the dragon representative, so what the fuck is going on?" Abigail looked at me like she had sprouted a second head and started to spit acid then broke down into hysterical laughter at my outburst. While this was taking place, Gudmundur sat in silence with a good-natured smile, acting as though nothing out of the ordinary had taken place.

Once Abigail and I had got our respective emotions under control, Gudmundur started by saying, "Ladies, welcome to my home. Abigail, as always, it is a pleasure to see you again, and I hope you are well. Lady Jessica, I don't believe I have had the pleasure of meeting you, but I believe we shall get along quite well. I understand that you haven't had the best experience with the dragon breed, but I must assure you that I am not like the others you have met. Now, from what I can understand, you have a very strange case on your hands. How can I be of assistance to you?" Well, this was turning into a day full of surprises. First, the cheery vampire that wants to help, and now a dragon breed? Something was going on, and I didn't like it.

"Why are you both so willing to help me? Every experience I've had that has had any dealing with your factions has always resulted in more hassle. As far as I've ever known, your two factions don't get along. You're both secretive bastards and hate helping anyone unless it benefits you, so spill, what's going on?" This time, it was Abigail that answered. "Jessica, being one of the dragon blood means you have some unique abilities. We know what some of these are enhanced senses, enhanced strength, and stamina, wounds that should take weeks or months to heal for you to heal in hours or at worse days. Am I right so far?"

At this, I just gave a nod of confirmation. She took this as a confirmation to continue and went on, "We also know that you have stopped ageing, and have a slew of other abilities that are none of my concern, but you have one that at this moment will help you a great deal. You know when and who to trust. It's like a sixth sense, a little itch at the back of your head that guides your decisions. What have these feelings been telling you?" I hated to admit it, but I do get feelings about people and situations and at the moment, it screamed that these are good people who mean me no harm.

"Fine, I will give you both the benefit of the doubt, but I warn you now, don't cross me! If your plan is to betray me, I will hunt you down and destroy you, do I make myself clear?"

"We understand, Lady Jessica, on my honour, I will do you no harm and will lay my life down in your service."

"That's a little extreme but I appreciate your enthusiasm. Now please tell me, what do we know about this case? Do either of you have any actionable intel that we can use to stop who or whatever is doing this?" "Um, no, we don't have anything, but I would love to have a rundown on the information you haveso far and maybe visit the crime scene if that would be at all possible. Wouldn't you agree, Abigail?"

"I agree. Seeing the site would definitely help. Should we head there now?"

Damn, these guys are eager. "No, we can't head there. I need to head back to the agency and get updates from the team, check on Alisha, and before you say you will head there without me, you can't. You don't

have clearance and I can't deal with the headache of you breaking into a crime scene. You have a choice. You can stay here and I can contact you later to meet me at the crime scene, or you can join me while I dowhat I need to do." They glanced at each other in a meaningful way, and both said, *we will stay with you*. "In that case, can we get some food before the drive back? I have a feeling it is going to be a long day, and I need coffee before I get grumpy."

Abigail turned to me with wide eyes and said while giggling, "What are you saying? We haven't seen you grumpy yet? Gudmundur, gets this woman coffee, stat." *Sarcastic little bloodsucker.* If I didn't need to cooperate with these idiots, I would kick them.

Chapter 9

Driving back to the agency was an interesting experience. The vampire and dragon in my back seat were like teenage girls with all the gossiping and giggling. Well, Gudmundur didn't exactly giggle. He actually had an infectious belly laugh, which was extremely annoying as it was ruining my hard-ass image every time I smiled. We approached the agency and could see there were a few police cars at the front of the building.

I parked next to the police cars and ran up the front steps. I could hear raised voices. "What the fuck is happening now?" I rushed in to see what was going on and was faced with Mini as she was yelling expletives at the top of her lungs, her face was bright red and I'm sure the vein in her temple was about to explode. I was wondering what could have pissed her off this badly, she was always so chilled out, then I saw the source of her rage, Detective Duncan Lancaster, and standing with him were two stuck up looking bureaucrats, one of which was holding Alisha's hand, and the kid looked as though she had been crying. A haze of red fell over me as I growled. Before anyone knew what was going on, my fist connected with Lancaster's jaw and he went down hard. Before I could continue my assault on the jackass that made a child cry, Gudmundur and Abigail grabbed me under both arms and struggled to remove me from the situation. They dragged me to a vacant office to cool down. I'm fairly sure at some point in the struggle, I may have roared. Once everyone calmed down, I was taken to the head of the London office while everyone else tried to clean up my mess, the imposing figure sat behind his desk, his fingers laced together. He leaned forward. "You must be the young lady that added to the commotion in the lobby. May I ask what it was you thought you were doing? That was a police officer you struck. I know you can't always control your temper and that sometimes you react without thinking, but I can't think what in that situation warrants your reaction?"

I let out a long breath and began trying to explain myself. "First, it was Mini! She was a little agitated by whatever was happening, and then I saw Alisha had been crying and that set me off. I had a run-in with the detective at the crime scene last night, so he ended up the target of my rage. What was happening there, anyway? When we arrived, Mini looked as though the world was ending and everyone was shouting."

The large man leaned back in his seat and took a deep breath. "That isn't really all that straightforward, child services wanted to take the child into custody until a family member had been tracked down. The detective wanted us to retain wardenship, as he believes that she could be a crucial witness and may still be able to help close this case. He also made a case that having her in unfamiliar surroundings with people she doesn't trust would be damaging to her after what she has witnessed."

It just suddenly dawned on me what that could mean for the case and for Alisha. The shock must have shown on my face because the boss added, "Do not worry, Jessica, the child will remain with Minerva for the duration of the case, and we will re-assess the situation then. Relief flooded my muscles. As they relaxed I physically slumped in the chair.

"The detective wasn't here to discuss the girl, it was just a happy coincidence that he arrived at the same time as child services also wanted to see if your meetings provided any useful leads, and if you have any updates on what's happening with the case. Do you have anything to go on at this point?"

"I haven't had any developments on the case, but both the vampires and the dragon breed have shown an interest, and I brought representatives from both with me to see if they can be useful. Also, I haven't had time to do a debrief with any of the team yet. I intended to gather everyone in the conference room now and see if anyone has made any progress."

"In that case, I won't keep you, but please, Jessica, try to remain in control of that temper and keep me appraised of your progress." At the dismissal, I rushed from his office like my hair was on fire and fled to the conference room where everyone was waiting for me, including the detective who was holding an ice pack to his already bruised jaw. I motioned for Alisha to come to speak to me out in the hall. She was accompanied by the child welfare agents. "Hey, Alisha, do you remember me from last night?" At this, she nodded. "I am going to be speaking to everyone about what happened so that we can catch whoever was responsible, and I would rather you not be in there, so would it be okay if I asked you to wait across the hall with these two agents?

She nodded again but gave me a quick smile, then I leaned in and whispered that the room had a vending machine that she was free to use, and if she asked the agents that would sit with her, they might let her get a few bits from it, but only if she was good and willing to share. The look of delight that lit her face was gone in seconds and was replaced with her retreating figure as she ran to waiting area. I gave the agents an apologetic look because that machine was a sugar addict's dream. Oh well, the kid deserved to indulge her sweet tooth. I got up and said to the agent that if they would be patient I would be happy to discuss the situation of Alisha's welfare with them after my meeting, and I would be very appreciative if they could wait with Alisha in the waiting area. They agreed with my request without a second thought and followed Alisha. Making my way back to the conference room, I had to mend fences and get everyone organised. I took my seat and the general chatter in the room died down. All eyes turned to me. "Everyone, I would like to apologise about my behaviour. The detective, I shouldn't have struck you, it was out of line. I understand you are here for an update on our investigation, but we don't have anything to report just yet, but I will contact you as soon as we have any leads. Do you have anything to report to me?"

Detective Lancaster removed the ice pack from the side of his jaw. "I don't have any more information about the case, but I heard someone at the station had notified child protective services, and I wanted to give your team the heads up."

"Well, I now feel like a complete idiot for overreacting the way I did. I hope you will accept my apology," "Well, you seem to be busy, and I have other cases needing my attention so if I hear anything I'll let you know and I hope you will do the same."

He then left, saying a few farewells to those who had gathered.

"Okay, now that's all dealt with, I feel like I need to

apologise to everyone, that waS unprofessional of me. Nothing I can say will justify my actions, but when I saw a Mini upset, and that Alisha had been upset, it triggered flashbacks to the cave. I promise I will try to keep better control of my emotions going forward." As I finished with my apology, Keith stood and addressed the room. "I have made some discoveries about Mr. Silver, Alisha's father. He wasn't just an innocent bystander. He was a lawyer that has defended some major scumbags. We think this was a statement killing. I'm not sure who ordered it, but I do know that a half-dozen men that Mr. Silver defended have been reported as missing, and we have another body that was discovered mutilated a few weeks ago, but we haven't been able to identify who it was. I have requested the M.E report and I will get it to you as soon as it arrives, I'm going to shake down some of my informants and if I get anything you will be the first to know."

"Okay that gives us something to go on. This could be some sort of turf war. We need to know more about these missing people, and the other body. Keith, can you continue looking into that? Also, the detective informed me that they have had a series of vagrants disappear, and a lot of mysterious deaths in the last 18 months. I will forward all the details, but I think they might be connected. Did you find anything from the mage's council?"

"Fortunately, they haven't admitted that they've had

anyone go missing, and only the usual sort of brawls that happen. They have noticed odd magic residue around the city. I have asked them to give us a list of these with the corresponding date and time. They should email us the data anytime now. That being said, they won't supply any help if things go sideways, but that's not surprising. I will try to collate all the data and work with the lab techs and Mini to see if we can see a pattern in the chaos."

I loved having Keith on our side. If anyone could find the common denominator, I hoped it was him. "What about anything from the Silver residents? I didn't really get a chance to look at the scene when I was there. Can anyone shed any light on what happened?"

Keith continued his report. "The autopsy on Mr. Silver still needs to be finished, but the other two have been done, and judging by the initial findings, I'm fairly confident that the results will be the same. The victims were alive, and they knew what was happening to them. It seems that some form of paralytic was realised into the Silver's home which incapacitated them while they were watching each other getting mutilated and devoured alive. I can confirm that Mr. Silver was the last to die, and it would appear that the perpetrator was interrupted in what it was doing. My reasoning for this is that as well as the flesh being torn from the body, they were also missing their hearts, and Mr. Silver was not. Also, the M.E have found traces of hair that they are fairly certain is not human. They haven't been able to establish what it isyet, but they are running a full database search to see if we get any hits. I think the child may have seen a lot more than we thought and she fled to that cupboard when the person responsible left. I advise that we handle questioning her very carefully."

We had only just started the meeting, and I was already getting a migraine.

While I was processing what Keith was saying, our little vampire guest interrupted. "The shifter council is reluctant to admit it has any problems and won't speak to you because they are paranoid and don't want to appear weak. I have reliable information that has had several pack members go missing over the past few weeks. Normally, this wouldn't be all that concerning as shifters go into the local woods or mountains all the time and lose themselves to their inner beast. When they are like this, weeks can pass without them realising it. But according to my contact, a young couple have gone missing and they are expecting a child. They have missed two appointments with a pack doctor, and this has the senior members of the pack nervous. They are reluctant to offer the packs cooperation because they fear someone is targeting them and don't wish to paint a bigger target on their backs."

Great, just what we need, paranoid and panicked shifters. "Mini, have you had a chance to speak to Alisha yet?"

"Not really, we've managed to get her cleaned up, and she's had a little breakfast, but she is still very wary of everyone. I can feel so much fear and terror radiating from the poor child. I will admit that the two of us losing our collective temper probably didn't help, but I did feel a slight amount of amusement from her when you hit the detective!"

I get the feeling I'm not going to live that down for a while. "Can you tell if Keith is on the right lines that she witnessed everything?"

"From the general feel I'm getting from her, I would say he's spot on, but I will require some time with her to be sure, I think it's a good idea that she stays within the confines of the agency until all this is resolved."

"That's fine by me. I will leave her in your care and to forewarn you, I told her about the free vending machine of sugary snacks."

I then set my sights on Abigail and Gudmundur. "Both of your factions are notorious for not cooperating with any law enforcement of any kind, and when you do decide to help, it is usually too late. Then there is the fact that you are sitting there like best friends! Everything I know about dragon breeds and vampires says that putting them in the same room together will usually end in threats of violence, if not actual violence, so what the fuck is going on? I don't want to hear that you just want to play nice and help. I'm not buying it."

Gudmundur sat straighter and cleared his voice, then said, "I apologise for any misunderstanding we may have caused you, Lady Jessica. We have no pertinent information on your current case. We are, however, more than happy to assist in helping you solve this case and once it is complete, we would request some of your time to help us with a very delicate situation. As you have mentioned, Abigail and I have a unique friendship, we have known each other for a few hundred years, but we will explain more of that later. I can, however, shed some light on what may have caused the deaths of the child's family, but it must be under someone's control, because if it wasn't, it would have left a trail of dead in its wake." "Gudmundur, what are we looking for?"

"I believe it is a Wendigo, and unless I'm incorrect, it is a freshly made one. You see, a Wendigo isn't summoned in the traditional sort of the way a normal spirit would, and it isn't a natural-born demon or monster like say, a dragon is. A Wendigo chooses to descend into darkness and evil. It starts by eating human flesh. The act of cannibalism is enough to draw the attention of an evil spirit that will whisper encouragement to the cannibal, and the more human flesh it consumes, the hungrier they become. The Wendigo is seen as the embodiment of gluttony, greed, and excess. They are never satisfied after killing and consuming one person. They are constantly searching for new victims. Wendigos are portrayed as simultaneously gluttonous and extremely thin due to starvation. Whenever a Wendigo eats its victim, it will grow in proportion to the meal it has eaten, so it can never be full, this is why a Wendigo will be gaunt to the point of emaciation. Its desiccated skin will be pulled tightly over its bones. With its bones pushing out against its skin, its complexion, the ash-grey of death, and its eyes pushed back deep into its sockets, the Wendigo will look like a gaunt skeleton recently disinterred from the grave. It will give off a strange and eerie odour of decay, decomposition, death, and corruption."

My jaw hit the floor. "You sat through this whole meeting when you knew what we were facing, and this is the first time you thought to mention it?"

"Well, you didn't ask."

Damn, he had a point.

"Okay, well, at least we now know what's doing the killing. What we need to know is why and who the hell is controlling it. I'm going to head back to the crime scene and see if I can find anything new. I'm guessing you two still want to check out the scene with me." At this they both nodded.

"Mini, I'm going to need you to tread carefully with Alisha. Before everyone heads off, I want you to call me the minute you get any leads. There is too much riding on this."

Everyone got up and began heading off to follow

their leads.

I asked Gudmundur and Abigail to wait in the conference room while I spoke to Alisha and child welfare. Mini accompanied me, and we satisfied the agents that Alisha was in good hands with us for the duration of the case. Before I left the waiting area to meet Gudmundur and Abigail in the conference room, I asked Mini if she had picked anything up from my two guests.

"They are keeping their emotions in check, but they have leaked a little. They find you amusing at times and are intrigued by you and your reactions. I don't think they mean you any harm. If anything, I pick up that they wish to protect you." *What, why would they want to protect me?* I was reasonably sure that the dragon breed would celebrate if I ever died, and I had no idea why the vamps would care what happened to me. Well, that was going to have to be a mystery for another day. "Mini I need you to work with Alisha and try to get me any details you can as to why anyone would want to do this to her family and if she can give us any details on the attack." Mini went back to sit with Alisha and they both began to talk in earnest. I went to the conference room to collect my two new friends and as I entered, they became eerily silent, I gave them a look and said, "I know you two are up to something. I don't know what it is, and if I'm honest, I don't really care. Just give me your word that you will do nothing to impede this investigation, and if you can, then assist me so that no one else dies. That would be great." Again, they glance at each other for the briefest of moments, and Abigail responds with, "We will assist you on the condition that once this case is solved, you will sit with us. We have much to discuss with you." *Great, another headache I didn't need.* "Okay, fine. Case first, then I deal with you two. I'm heading back to the Silver's home. There has to be something that we are missing."

Chapter 10

Pulling up to the Silver's house and seeing the police tape and the patrol car turned my stomach. I approached the officer to show him my credentials, but he had already been told I was coming. I motioned for Gudmundur and Abigail to join me. When I ducked under the cordoned building, upon opening the door I was hit with the stale smell of blood and fear. Walking into the living area sent a shiver down my spine. It was as if the fear and terror was a tangible force that was assaulting every single one of my senses. Gudmundur and Abigail were surveying the home behind me, being careful not to disturb anything, but taking in every detail as they went. I asked out loud, "Call out anything you see as you see it. I'm assuming you have both done this sort of thing before." I got affirmative grunts from both of them. Abigail shouted, "Where was Alisha found?" This struck me as an odd question, because I was sure I had told them she was found in the wine cellar cowering

133

and swinging a knife. "She was in the wine cellar. Why do you ask?"

"I'm picking up her scent. From what I'm smelling, she ran to the cellar when she heard sirens from the police."

"What do you mean? I got here after the police, but the kid was in there. She was scared out of her mind." "What I'm saying is that there is more going on here than we think." I couldn't disagree with her

—things aren't exactly adding up. "Okay, keep looking. I think Mr. Silver must have seen something during his work that warranted his boss to do this. He has an office downstairs, so I'm going to head there and look for any files or papers that might link to his work. Also, see if you can find any computers or laptops that we can search." We tore through every inch of the house, garden, and garage. It took hours, but we found some documents that seemed promising about some containers that were supposed to be heading for a warehouse. Judging by what I could see, the documents we found contained all sorts of falsified reports. It looked like another container was due for delivery—this must be what we are looking for. I looked to Gudmundur and Abigail, who had been reading the documents over my shoulder. "Well, do you think it's worth checking out the warehouse location to see if this is connected to the case, or should we pass it on to the officer out the front?" Abigail gave me a toothy smile.

"Well, we all know the police force is overworked, so why don't we take care of this little stakeout? I only have two questions before we leave. First is to you, Gudmundur. Do you sell blood at The Dragon's Keep?" I gasped in horror. Surely she didn't think the place we met him at would serve blood. Gudmundur replied good-naturedly, " I have only had the establishment for very short time as you know, sweetest Abigail, but I have ensured that we have a few bottles of types A, B, AB, and O. One of the witches that I employ is working on a process to flavour the blood as well, so you will have that to look forward to if you become one of my regular clients."

"What the hell, please don't tell me you go out and bleed people so you can bottle blood and sell it for a profit." I could feel the heat rising as I got angrier, and the air began to crackle, like it had gained an electrical charge. *Shit, I need to get my temper under control.* I started to take deep, calming breaths, and I heard Gudmundur explain that he did not condone anyone using humans that way, but vampires do need human blood to live. However, they had found that humans will give blood freely if they are given money in exchange for it.

"So, to say it simply, we pay humans to donate blood. We never take too much, and we ensure that they have a meal before they leave our supervision. I believe the vampire council enforces something similar and those who choose to kill humans for blood are classed as renegades, hunted and put down." Hearing this managed to calm me down. I looked at them both and was about to apologise for my overreaction when the little blood sucker burst out in uncontrollable laughter. "Wow, you really are amazing. Everything I've heard about you is true. You punch first and ask questions later, but really, you need to control that temper, especially if you don't understand the supernatural world more fully."

I grumbled under my breath. "Yeah, I guess I just kinda freaked out a little when you said you sold blood. I apologise."

"Okay, now we have that cleared up, do you have all the surveillance equipment you think we will need at the agency?"

"Yes, we have all the latest tech and a fully stocked armoury. I can drop you both at The Dragon's Keep, then get what we need at the agency and meet you when you're done!"

"No, you will come to The Dragons Keep. You will eat, and don't worry about any supplies. Just tell me anything you specifically require and I will have it." Gudmundur stated this like it was nothing of consequence. These two might be bigger deals than I originally thought. They carry themselves with a confidence that I have only seen in the boss. I think I may have a few questions for these two while we prepare for what is to come.

***

I parked near the entrance of The Dragon's Keep. It seemed to be just as busy as when we were there earlier that day. We entered and saw the same waitress as this morning, who showed us to the same table we used. Gudmundur asked her to bring two bottles of 2009 Chateau Petrus and a warm bottle of the top shelf special, as well as three glasses. She rushed off to for fill his request, and Abigail pointed a finger at him saying, "Pulling out all the stops with that wine, aren't you? That stuff isn't cheap, even with your type of customers, I doubt their pockets run that deep."

"It's actually from my own collection. I have been told that Lady Jessica likes to partake of a glass of red wine, and this one is a particular favourite of mine. I have also been told that it goes very nicely when mixed with type O, and was hoping you would join us while we eat and create strategies for our reconnaissance mission. Now, before we order food, I would like to know of any equipment that you believe we may need?" This is where I jumped in. I had been trying to think of everything we might need while not having to carry a lot of equipment, so we can still be manoeuvrable. But before I gave him the list of equipment, I needed to know what my two companions are capable of. "I have an idea of what we need, but I need information on your capabilities first. You're up, Gudmundur. What are your experiences, and what do you bring to the operation?"

"You are wise to ask. Very well. I have taken part in numerous wars and battles in my long years in both my dragon and human shapes, but in our current situation, I would say I have taken part in many of the human wars that have taken place over the last one hundred years. I've been in World War One and World War Two, the Korean War, the Vietnam war, and the Gulf War. In most of these conflicts, I have been used for covert operations. I can use most modern weapons surveillance equipment and communication systems. As for my personal attributes, as you can imagine, I am stronger and faster than any human, and even most but the oldest vampires. I am an ice dragon, so I have some influence over ice and frost. I do also have a little bit of talent with compulsion, but I'm sure Abigail is better at that than I am, aren't you?"

"Well, he's got me there. I am much better at tinkering with people's minds than the big guy is." *Wow, note to self, don't piss this guy off.* "Okay, Abigail, you're up. What do you bring to the party?"

"I'm happy you asked. Well, all my senses are heightened, so I can usually tell when I'm being lied to just by hearing people's heartbeat or by the fluctuations in their temperature. It also makes me an expert tracker. I can use most firearms available, but I prefer to use blades. I can also elongate my finger nails into claws that are sharper and more durable than most other blades. I also have better than normal strength speed and stamina. Unfortunately, I can't use magic or anything like that." Fuck me, these two are like a walking arsenal. I now need to remove most of the items from my shopping list. That will makeus lighter and more stealth like.

"Okay, in that case, we should need tactical fatigues for all of us, plus light side arms. L9A1 browning would be a good choice if you have any, or an SA80 would be better. We would also need a night and thermal vision system, and standard comms for if we get separated. Oh, and if you have any tactical blades that would be fantastic. Do you think you can get what we need?" Before anyone could respond tomy question, our waitress appeared from nowhere and placed three glasses in front of us and put the bottles in the centre of our table. She then straightened and pulled out a digital tablet and asked if we would like to order something to eat. Before I could answer, my stomach growled, alerting everyone at the table that I was famished. "I would like to order the biggest steak on the menu with baked potatoes, seasonal vegetables and peppercorn sauce." Gudmundur just shrugged as though that was a normal order and said he would have his usual, and asked her to send out his assistant, Max. A moment later, a boy no older than 18 and of a slight build came out to our table. He bowed slightly and said, " My lord, how canI help you?"

"Max, I would like to introduce you to Lady Jessica, and a good friend of mine, Abigail. I need you to assemble a vehicle loaded with the following items." As he listed the things we needed to Max, I noticed that Max was glaring at me as though I was something disgusting at the bottom of his shoe. *Well, that is the sort of behaviour I have been told to expect from the dragon breed.* "Max, is there something you wish to say?" Max focused his attention back to Gudmundur and something he saw in Gudmundur's eyes made him go a shade paler.

"My lord, I mean no offence, but it is the abomination. It should not be allowed to live, and you should not be forced to be in its company." Before anyone could blink and so silently that no one else in the pub had noticed, Max was bent forward so that it looked as though he and Gudmundur were exchanging a quiet word, but from where I sat, I could see the look of fear on Maxs face. As Gudmundur held him by his collar, he pulled him close as his right arm became covered in interlocking scales and his hand became claws. He flashed his newly formed claws in front of Max's face, and with a deep growl said, "If you disrespect Lady Jessica again and I hear of it, I will kill you. Do I make myself clear?"

Shaking with fear and with eyes as large as dish plates, Max nodded slowly. "Very well, you have a task to do, so get out of my sight. And do it!" If I didn't know better, I would have thought that Max pissed himself in fear. "

"That really wasn't necessary. I have been prewarned that I should expect this sort of behaviour from the dragon breed. I will admit that it pisses me off, but if they don't physically hurt me, I will survive." What I didn't say is that the comments and looks hurt me deeply. It wasn't my fault that some psycho pumped me full of dragon blood. I didn't ask for it, and I didn't need a bunch of self-important twat waffles to give me shit about it.

"Lady Jessica, you do not deserve to be treated in such a way. You were dealt a very harsh hand and the way you have conducted yourself is above reproach, I apologise for how the dragon breed have treated you, but I can assure you that the behaviour and thoughts of those like Max do not represent the thoughts and feelings of the majority." As he finished speaking, our food arrived, and I began to salivate. The food looked amazing. The thoughts going through my head must have shown on my face, because Abigail spoke up and said, "Are you going to eat that wonderful meal, or are you just going to make love to it with your eyes?" At her question, I could feel the heat on my cheeks as I blushed and then dove into my meal, enjoying the wine as I ate.

It didn't take us long to finish our delicious meal. I was going to need to come here again. We had discussed our plan of action, and as we were preparing to leave, my phone started to ring. Looking at the caller I.D, it showed it was Mini. I picked it up as the others gathered their gear and I followed them to the back of the pub. "Yeah, Mini, what's up?"

"Hey, I've just finished talking with Alisha. What those bastards did... It's disgusting. They arrived as the family were having dinner and relaxing for the evening. All she can say is a monster came through. As soon as she saw it—as soon as they all saw it— they were paralysed in fear. She explained that she tried to call out, but couldn't. She heard the monster say they would make her mother watch. Then a man walked in behind the monster and placed a hand on the beast's shoulder and it calmed immediately, like a dog obeying a masters silent command. Then he scolded the beast like a parent would a child and said the mother would be first, then the brother then. He would question the father, but the girl was too valuable, that they had already given her some of the compound and she hadn't showed any rejection, so they would take the girl with them to join the rest of their little army. Once he had his speech, he set the beast on the mother and brother, and all she could do was watch and sob. When they got to her father, they went slow and made sure he suffered. They questioned him and tore him apart. Alisha couldn't remember what they asked. I think she had gone in to shock. The next thing she knew, the man approached her to try and drag her from the house, but there was something going on and she fought back and ran. That's why she lashed out with that knife. The door opened, and she was faced with a man, I would have done the same in her position."

I didn't know what to say. Just hearing the abridged version was enough to shock me so much I was nearly throwing up my meal, but Minerva hadn't finished. "Jess, it's worse than you think. When she told me about the compound, I asked for the lab to draw some blood. It's like yours. It shows the same sort of anomalies, just not as potent. Jess, what are you planning to do?"

"Sorry, Mini. I need to go kick a dragon in the balls." Before she could reply, I had hung up. At the mention of kicking a dragon in his family jewels, Abigail and Gudmundur began to turn to see what I was talking about. Abigail jumped out of harm's way before my fist collided with Gudmundur's jaw. "You son of a bitch, was she the reason you wanted to be on the case? How many have you cunts created?" As he started to get up from my first hit, I aimed a kick at his head, hoping to get a good hit in to jog his memory, but he blocked so fast I didn't see what happened. He then pulled my other leg out from under me, forcing me to fall in a heap on my ass. Then he pinned me. I faintly heard Abigail giggle in the background. *I swear when I get up and finish kicking the dragon's ass, I will kick her ass for laughing.* "What do you think you 're doing, Jessica?"

"You have some nerve asking me that. How many have you idiots given blood to? How many haven't made the change and died in agony so you can have your own little army?"

"I don't know what you 're talking about, but if you

calm down, I will try to help."

"I've just got off the phone with the agency. I have been informed that Alisha has the same type of anomalies in her blood as I do, so explain how you don't know anything about this. How many dragons go around shoving their blood into kids?"

The look on his face could freeze the blood. "I have already told you, we don't do that sort of thing. The last time it happened, it cost too many lives. Are you sure of the results?"

"I'm about as sure as I can be. Why?"

"Would you object to someone from the council meeting with the child and looking at her blood results so that we can figure out what's happening?"

I took a second to consider his proposal. "Okay, make the arrangements, but if anything happens to her, I will be holding you responsible."

He nodded his agreement and moved away from me, lifting his phone to speak. Whatever he was saying, it was clear from his body language that he was pissed. After a few minutes of heated conversation, he turned back to me, hanging up on whoever he was speaking to.

"One of the medics from the council will be heading out to assess her condition. It will be someone I know, and I promise they will treat her well."

"Fine, let's get going. We are already running behind schedule," I said to the vampire and dragon as I grabbed my gear and headed for the car.

Chapter 11

We were set up one mile from the perimeter of the warehouse and had been carrying out standard surveillance for the past few hours. In near silence, I was dividing my time between thinking of the mission and being concerned for Alisha. I needed to get my head on straight. We had decided to breach when the container arrived, and all attention would be on the main gate receiving the container. The security was some of the best I had ever seen. They had biometric scanners at all access points, several roaming patrols, and all of the guards seemed to be heavily armed. On the bright side for us, they appeared to be humans. So a few subtle compulsions and a little stealth should be all we need to infiltrate the site. Our plan was simple: infiltrate, take photo evidence of anything we see, locate a paper trail or physical pieces of evidence to figure out everything that was happening, confirm the contents of the container and get out all of this. We wanted to achieve all of this without drawing attention to ourselves. I really hoped the powers that be had our backs on this one.

Abigail caught my attention to notify me that the container truck was on its way and we needed to move. As per the plan, we went on foot to the opposite side of the compound. Abigail and Gudmundur could scale the fence without problems. I needed help, so as agreed earlier, I was scooped up in the dragon's arms like a bride being carried in over the threshold of a room, except he leapt a fence that was at least 20ft high. We landed on the other side as though it was nothing. He put me back on my feet, and we proceeded to gain access to the building through the side entrance. We had to time our entrance between patrols. Abigail went first to make sure the coast was clear, and with in seconds, we were in undetected. But the view that was created was nothing like I expected. They had rows and rows of military-style cots set out like a hospital tent in some war zone, but instead of wounded soldiers, I saw children, rows upon rows of children laying unconscious in these cots, all with IV leads and oxygen masks attached to them. What the hell was going on? Abigail brought my attention to the task at hand and lead us to a staircase that seemed to lead to the next level, where we saw lot of the same and a few heavily pregnant women and young men. None of them appeared older than their early twenties. There was also what seemed to be an office and a lab area walled off. We headed straight for the office. Once inside, I whispered for them to search the place as fast as possible and photograph anything and everything they could. They got to work quickly and efficiently. You could tell they had done this before. I watched our point of exit, not wanting to be caught on the back foot if someone came in here. In minutes we were out the door and heading for the lab. Luck was sticking with us as we encountered zero opposition. They must have had all hands dealing with the container, which worked out great for us. We entered the lab and went straight for the bank of computers, indicating for Gudmundur to cover the exit. I motioned for Abigail to get some samples if possible, but she was already doing it. I focused on the computers in front of me. All seemedto be networked, so I slid my pen drive in and entered my command code to clone the computer and install backdoor administrative accesses to us. The tense part of the operation was waiting for the notification telling me the upload had been complete. As the light turned green and the computer notified us that the action was complete, I singled to the others to move out. We just needed to get our eyes on the shipping container and find out what they were hauling. We exited the building the way we came, avoiding the roaming guards and getting as many pictures of the kids laid out on the cots as possible.

Back on the ground level, we made our way to the loading area. There was still a buzz of activity. From our, positions we could see that they were unloading more children from the containers, all of them looking scared, dirty, and malnourished. But that wasn't the only thing. As the children are led to what looked like a decontamination area that was sealed off by some sort of plexiglass, the workers start to unload secured containers, all marked as hazardous.

Well, isn't this interesting. We have a container full of kids with what looks to be a fuck tonne of hazardous waste being brought to a facility full of unconscious children linked up to life support. I really don't like where this investigation is going. I signal to Gudmundur and Abigail to say we need to get out of here and debrief at the agency.

We make our way out of the facility without alerting anyone to our presence. Back at the car, we load up our gear as quickly and quietly as we can. I couldn't bring myself to say anything to the others about what we saw in that facility, and I got the impression that the other two didn't want to broach the subject, so once we loaded up, we drove back to the agency in silence, each alone with our own thoughts.

Chapter 12

Back at the agency, Gudmundur and Abigail helped me put together briefings for the entire team. It was boring office work, but it kept us busy while we waited for everyone to arrive. As I put the finishing touches on the files, Gudmundur walked in with a tray full of coffee for everyone. As the dark aroma from the coffee hit me, I realised how long it had been since I had slept, and I was momentarily overcome with bone-deep exhaustion. *Well, there is no rest for the wicked.* "Thanks, dragon boy. I needed this. Just make sure you keep it coming." Not long after I finished my coffee, everyone began to arrive. Abigail, Gudmundur, and I remained fairly silent while everyone took a seat. By the looks people were giving each other, I could only assume that everyone had information for me, and I wasn't going to like it. "Okay, everyone, I'm going to outline what we have so far. Then you can ask questions or contribute whatever information you have ascertained."

After a quick outline, I asked Keith and Mini if they had any update on Alisha's blood. They both looked at me a little nervously, then Mini spoke, "Sweetie, we need you to sit down and try not to react while we call in Gudmundur's associate. You are not going to like what he has to say, but we need you to remain calm. Can you do that for us?" Just looking at them, I could tell it was the worst news, but I nodded to give them my word that I would remain calm.

I took a deep, calming breath and gripped the metal armrest of my chair, focusing all the tension in my body into maintaining an iron grip on the armrests so I wouldn't lash out. Mini showed in a very thin man into the conference room and first impressions would have you thinking he was a typical bookworm with his glasses worn askew, his hair tousled, shirt untucked from his jeans, and the general appearance that he had been lost in his research for days on end and wouldn't be able to tell you the time or day of the week. But when his gaze landed on you, you could feel him stripping you down to your core and analysing your every movement and gesture. This guy was truly an apex predator, just one look into his eyes, and you could feel they contained violence just waiting to be unleashed upon his enemies.

"Greetings, everyone. I am Ogma. As you are aware, I am here at the request of Gudmundur to do an assessment on young miss Alisha, and to see if she has been infused with dragon blood. I can confirm that the child is one of the marked and she has been infused with dragon blood. However, it has not been done traditionally." We all stared at him as though he was speaking a foreign language. "As Lady Jessica has experienced personally, the process of making a warrior of the dragon blood is painful and the majority of the time is fatal. The reason for this is that we dragons are overflowing with magical energy and power. Humans, for the most part, have very little magical ability, and although there are exceptions, those who bear a dragon mark are never born with any magical abilities, so introducing all this power burns out the human vessel and kills them. But when a dragon dies, the magic in its blood and tissue degrades over time and the remains don't decompose as rapidly as most other living things. It can take centuries for the remains and the magic to deteriorate to the point that they are worthless. I believe what has been done to Alisha and the rest of the children you have located. They have been injected with dead dragon tissue and blood. The results of Alisha's blood shows a degree of necrosis in the foreign cells, and a much lower concentration of magical power than I would have expected."

"So what does this mean? Is she one of the dragon blood like me, or will it work its way out of her system?"

"From what I can see, her system has already adapted to the blood, and changes have taken place that are irreversible. She probably experienced cold or flu-like symptoms while these changes took place, so she avoided the days of torturous pain that you experienced. The changes that she is experiencing are only slight at this point, but I believe in the fullness of time, she will experience more dramatic manifestations of her newfound power. What I would like to do is take Alisha into my care so that I can guide her so that she isn't a threat to herself or others. I understand that until this investigation is over, you will need to keep her here so that she is protected, and I am happy to stay with her here to assist in her protection and also to help explain what might begin to happen to her in the future. I can also try to explain the supernatural world to her so she isn't so overwhelmed. My offer will still stand once your investigations are complete, and I will offer the same to anyone else who is being affected by this."

I took a moment to consider what he was saying. I looked around the table to see if anyone was about to object, but everyone seemed taken aback by what Ogma was suggesting, so I asked the only thing that came to mind. "And what do you get out of doing these children such kindness? In my experience, dragons very rarely do something out of the kindness of their hearts. Even Gudmundur and Abigail are only helping me in this case because they want to discuss something with me at the end of it." At the end of my statement, I glared at him with such intensity I would make most grown men cower.

"I see you distrust the dragon breed, and I know we deserve your mistrust. We have not treated you with kindness. and I know that even in my master's presences. you have suffered disrespect and outright hostility at the hands of my kind, but I can assure you that I harbour you no ill will and I will lay downmy life in the defence of these children. against any that would wish harm to them. Even if those wishing them harm are my kind, on that I give you my word." At his final word, I felt the magic in his speech. He wasn't just trying to convince me of his sincerity—he was giving me his oath in front of witnesses. My jaw was agape in shock then everyone at the table stood and chanted.

"On your word, we bear witness."

Shit, things just got very real, quick. "Okay, Ogma. I believe that you mean the children no harm and I will accept your offer to protect Alisha. Mini, if you have nothing left to report, would you be kind enough to accompany Ogma to Alisha and explain that he will be staying with her for a while and try tomake sure they get along?" I felt bad saddling Mini with this, but she was the best person at the office tomake sure everything went without a problem or any temper tantrums from the dragon or the young girl. Mini led the dragon out of the conference room, giving me a pointed look that told me she would makeme suffer for putting her on babysitting duties.

I moved on and asked Keith if he had anything from a forensic standpoint that might help us. He explained at length that he could back everything up that we had already come to and he would get his team on the recovered information from the warehouse and let me know if they come up with more intel about who might be pulling the strings. The rest of the meeting went on in the same way. The shifters knew something was going on, but didn't care as it didn't affect them and refused to get involved. But the mages surprised me. They had offered full cooperation and were already preparing to help in any way possible. They had already supplied us with information on how we might be able to subdue a Wendigo. Iasked Keith to follow up on that project and to gather the equipment and weapons we would need to take the beast down. He rushed out of the office with a gleam in his eyes at the thought of the fight to come.

I was left in the conference room with my two new shadows and the boss of the London office. I looked into his deep blue eyes. It was like staring into the abyss ,waiting for something, anything, to move. Before I became entranced and fell into those beautiful eyes forever, I had to mentally slap myself out of it.

"Sir, this case is getting worse with every turn, and we still haven't figured out who is behind it. We have gruesome murders, children being infused with the blood and the tissue of a dead dragon, a warehouse facility full of state-of-the-art medical experiments surrounded by trigger-happy mercenaries.

I don't know what to do next. Should I raid the building and rescue the kids? Should I hold back and see if we can get more information on the mastermind so we can take them down and shut down the whole operation? Who would have the resources available to be able to pull something like this off and why bother? What am I not seeing, and what should I do?"

"Jessica, you have a lot of questions and more paths in front of you than even I can see. What I think you should do is irrelevant. This is your case. It is your decision, and I will back your choice.

However, I think at this point you need rest and sleep. I know that isn't what you want to hear, but with rest comes clarity, and whatever road you choose to take, you will need to be at a hundred percent. So go back to the dorms and get some rest. I will tell the rest of the team to do the same. You are off the clock until tomorrow morning, at which time, I will expect to see you in my office with a plan of action for your next steps in this case."

The boss then stood and left without another word. I guess I needed to recharge, but it drove me crazy that children were out there being experimented on and I was being told to sleep and do nothing about it.

I motioned for Abigail and Gudmundur to follow me, and when we got to the hall, I dismissed them and said we could meet tomorrow at 8 a.m. to give us some time to plan before our meeting with the boss. I walked away, heading to the dorm rooms and fantasising about a glass of wine and a hot shower when I noticed Abigail was following me. I raised an eyebrow at her in question, and she merely shrugged, saying, "I'm not letting you out of my sight. Gudmundur is going to see if he can get anything more out of Ogma than he is going to inform the dragon council about what we have uncovered. He is going to be at the agency bright and early, and hopefully, he will have information that may affect the course of what you wish to do going forward."

"So what, are you going to be my bodyguard for the evening?" I asked in my most sarcastic tone.

She just replied with a laugh, saying, "I think I should be the one with a bodyguard to protect me from you. How about we just watch each other's backs while we rest up in your dorm?"

I just huffed. "Fine, let's get going." We reached the elevator and headed to my dorm.

Chapter 13

Back at my dorm room, I told Abigail to make herself at home, and if she wanted, I could arrange for her to have her own dorm room.

"No, I think I will be quite comfortable in here with you."

"Fine, suit yourself, but at least make yourself useful and see if they have any food. A glass of wine wouldn't go amiss either."

With that taken care of, I headed to the en-suite shower, locking the door behind me. I pressed my head against the door, taking in a deep breath and letting it out slowly. My head was spinning. I had so much going through my head. I hardly knew if I was coming or going. I started my shower in the hopes that the feel of hot water on my tired muscles would help me figure out what my next course of action would be. After too short a time in the shower, I headed to the kitchen to find my little vampire shadow holding a bottle of wine and two glasses.

"Well, damn, you work fast. Did you happen to magic any food, or are you just trying to get me drunk?"

"I ordered a pizza for you. It should be here shortly, but I thought I would join you for a glass of wine while we wait and maybe get to know each other a little better."

I took a moment to consider my options and thought to hell with it. If she was going to stick around, I might as well try to get some information out of her.

"Well, if you are going to hang around, do you wish to enlighten me about what your interests are in me while we have this little slumber party?" Abigail glanced at me as if what she was about to say would change the nature of the world and said, "Maybe I just enjoy your company. You are such an amusing person to be around. I haven't enjoyed myself this much in years."

"Really? Is that how you're going to play your hand? Fine, be cryptic if that's what you want. But once all this is over, I expect answers from you and that giant lizard." That being said, I headed to the lounge with Abigail following my lead. I got comfortable on a plush cuddle chair and she lounged on the sofa opposite me. I took a sip of my wine. "Well, if you aren't prepared to tell me why you're so interested in me, you can at least tell me your thoughts on the case."

"I think you're on the right track and locating the warehouse is going to give us a great opportunity to get the leads that we need on everyone involved. The shifters reluctance to get involved is concerning me. Word gets around fast in the supernatural communities. The fact that the agency has sent people to all factions and that Gudmundur and myself have involved ourselves so heavily should have been enough to get the shifters on board. My thoughts are that whoever is behind all this has either blackmailed the shifters, or is paying them as mercenaries. It's not uncommon for the packs to take on mercenary jobs, but I wouldn't think they would willingly take a job like this. I think you may want to ask any of the agency shifters to look at the local packs and try to find out what they know."

Before I could reply, there was a knock at the door. Great the food was here, and just in time too. I needed something to fill the void while I thought about what Abigail just said. Did she really believe that the shifters could be involved?

Opening the door revealed a delivery guy holding food. The smell of garlic, cheese, and spicy sausage from the pizza, the side of wings, and garlic bread had me salivating. I thanked the guy for the food and gave him a £20 as a tip. I always tip the delivery guys well so they remember my details and rush my orders to me. I headed into my lounge and set the boxes down before I started to dig in. I reached for my wineglass, only to find that

Abigail had topped it up for me. I may need to keep the bloodsucker around if she keeps my glass topped up.

"So, do you believe that we have shifter involvement in this case? I agree that their refusal to help is concerning, but they have people missing. Maybe they are looking into it discreetly, or the cases might be unrelated, and they just have their hands full." I wasn't expecting a response from the cheerful little vampire, but my statement seemed to have her thinking things through. While I had the chance, I picked the largest slice of pizza from the box and started to mull things over in my head.

We sat like this for a while in comparative silence, each occasionally reaching into a box to grab food while we thought. By the time the food was gone, we both had troubled expressions. Abigail spoke first, all former cheer vanished from her voice. "I need to make some calls to verify some of my suspicions. I'm also going to get a monitoring unit out to the warehouse ASAP. You need to get some rest. I will wake you in a few hours and brief you on anything I find."

At her brisk exit, I realised how tired I was and resigned myself to the fact that I needed sleep. Once I gotto my bed, I passed out when my head hit my pillow.

Chapter 14

The sound of raised voice woke me. It took me a moment to realise that it was Abigail and Gudmundur arguing with a third voice that I didn't recognise. I could make out a few words of what was going on, and it didn't sound like it would devolve into violence anytime soon, so I went to the en-suite, stripping my clothes, and got into hot a shower to hopefully help wake me up and give me the patience to deal with the heaping pile of shit that was going to get unloaded on my doorstep today. After spending as much time as I dared to get myself mentally prepared for the ensuing chaos that this case would probably bring, I dressed in loose fit tactical gear that to those unaware with my job would class as casual wear, but to those who knew me, I was in steel toe boots, lightweight combat pants and an under armour shirt and a loose fit hoody. I was carrying enough weapons to take out a small army. Now awake, armed and under-caffeinated, I took a step out of the bedroom to see the three figures whose voices woke me in the kitchen drinking coffee.

"So, does anyone want to tell me why I have a stranger in my dorm room raising his voice at an ungodly hour in the morning and drinking coffee or do I start cutting people's balls off first?" At my rather unfriendly morning greeting, the stranger and Gudmundur both turned with their mouths agape, lost for words. Whatever they saw on my face made the colour drain from them. True to form, Abigail just leaned against the counter and purred, "I'll get you a coffee, and dragon boy will introduce your guest. Please don't injure them."

I hate morning people. "Fine, I'll take it black with two brown sugars. While she is doing that, would one of you like to explain to me what's going on?" As I glared at both men, Gudmundur said, "My apologies, it was not my intention to cause you distress, but this is an envoy from the united packs of London. They wish to ask for your help as they believe a prominent child of one of the packs has been taken, and they feel it may be linked to your current case."

"They refuse to help us when we ask for help when we tell them that a kid has witnessed the horrific murder of her entire family, but they think they can just walk into my investigation and demand to be let on my case because some hotshot's kid goes missing? What aren't you telling me? Shifter kids go missing all the time."

"Let me introduce myself. I'm Milo, and I'm sorry for the intrusion, but I believe that the child in question has been taken by the same people as you are investigating. We received a message informing us that if we co-operated with the agency, we would never see the boy again, and our people would continue to vanish. The fact that I am here as an envoy of the united packs can not be made public. As it is, I am like your shifter colleagues. I'm not connected to any of the packs because I am a loner, so my involvement can not be held against them. For the convenience of cover, I work for Gudmundur."

"That all seems to make sense. So, what information do you have for us, or is it just that the packs are being strong-armed into staying away from this investigation?"

"I have a list of all those shifters we think have been abducted by these individuals, as well as reports that they are taking people from the streets. From the information I have been given and what I have been able to confirm from my own enquiries, they aren't only dragon marked. They are taking anyone they can, and not just children. The warehouse you infiltrated isn't the only site they have. I know of at least four others. Two seem to be research facilities and aren't holding any of the abducted, the other two seem to be testing grounds. The site you guys broke into seems to be where they take them after they have completed whatever they do at the testing grounds. I have attempted to trace who the buildings belong to, but they have been purchased through many shells and dummy corporations, and every lead I come up with leads me to a dead-end. That's why I'm here. I'm hoping that by working together, we might be able to stop this."

I gaze into his eyes, looking for a trace of deception, but all I can feel is seniority. "Okay, I appreciate the aid you offer. Has Gudmundur briefed you about what is currently happening, and about the girl, Alisha, who is currently under both the agency's and a dragon's protection?"

He nods, saying he has been briefed at this point. Abigail brings me my coffee, and it smells heavenly. I motion for everyone to take a seat. "So, Milo, how do you think the Silver family works into this? All we know is that Alisa has been infused, but we don't know when or how. We have lab techs going over all the evidence, but I don't think we are going to go get any leads from them anytime soon." They all signal their agreement. "While you have been doing your independent investigations, have you heard of them using a Wendigo?"

Milo nods. "Yes, I believe they tortured one of the subjects and feed it a diet of raw human flesh. I believe it was the subjects that didn't survive the experiments. From what I understand, they aren't just trying to create more dragon blood warriors, but they are trying to create their very own army of monsters."

I sat there, mouth agape at what I had just heard. This was worse than I had ever thought possible, but now I knew what I needed to do. Those bastards needed to be stopped, and the first step was to shut these facilities and find out who was behind this. It must have been someone with power and money and a lot of influence. I needed to get to the boss's office and round up the troops today. It was going to feel like an eternity, and I had a feeling that it was going to end in bloodshed.

Chapter 15

Briefing the boss was one of the most nerve-wracking things I had done in a while. After I outlined what we had found out and explained that I wanted to hit all the confirmed locations in synchronised raids, he looked at me, considering my proposal.

"I agree with your assessment, and I think a synchronised assault is a way forward. With all the information you have gathered, I can conclude that someone with high connections is behind this, so I want to get the raids done today so the plan can't be leaked. Even if it is, they won't have time to coordinate a plan to destroy evidence and flee. Before you go and start your preparations, I would like for you to wait here while I confide something."

Not waiting for my response, he left me alone in his office. Half an hour later, and I was starting to get impatient. I wanted to be doing something, to be planning or strategising or kicking down doors, anything other than sitting in an office like a school kid waiting to be scolded. Before much more time passed, I started to pace, attempting to calm my nervous energy. When the boss finally returned, he was joined by a tall, dark stranger and I think I must have dribbled. He was at least seven-foot tall, skin the colour of milkchocolate, the eyes a bright silver with dreadlocks down his back. He was wearing a silver-grey suit that hugged his body in all the right places. You could tell from looking that he didn't get his body from hitting the gym. The way he walked and moved suggested years of needing to use his body for survival. You see his type of body on seasoned martial artists and soldiers. He exchanged glances with me andgave me a knowing smirk, then moved over to the boss's sofa and lounged on it as though he didn't have a care in the world.

"Jess, I would like to introduce you to Enlil. He is from the watcher's council. The council has expressed concerns about what you have found, and Lord Enlil has volunteered to be our point of contact with the council."

The look I gave the pair of them must have been worse than I thought, because Lord Enlil spoke, "Don't concern yourself with my presence, child. I will interfere as a last resort. I have many reasons for coming to observe, and it has a small amount to do with your case. I have complete confidence that you will prevail and I look forward to hearing more than the case develops."

Okay, that was a shock. "Boss, if there is nothing else, I would like to brief the teams and start rolling out the operation to shut these facilities and find out what's truly happening."

"That's fine but I want to be patched into all communications, and I will run a backup command centre from here. Do you understand?"

"Yes, sir."

I headed out of the boss's office and went straight to the conference room that we had been using as our main base of operations. As I walked in, I could tell by the atmosphere that Gudmundur and Abigail had started to fill everyone in on what we had discovered.

Chapter 16

I needed to speak to Gudmundur and Abigail after we had done the planning and were on our way to the raid sites. The appearance of Enlil had me worried, and what was the watcher council's interest? *Maybe I should call Alex after the raid and ask him to shed some light on what seems to be going on,* I thought.

I needed to focus and get this done. Hopefully, by the end of the day, we should have a lot more to go on. I opened the door to the conference room and was faced with more people than I had expected. One of the monitors on the back wall also showed a video stream from the office I had just left. Sat bold as brass was Enlil and the boss. Everyone's attention was on me. I cleared my throat and took my seat.

"Some of you know who I am, but others don't. To make things clear, I am here to set up five raids on facilities that are responsible for kidnapping, murder, and experiments on those they have taken," I continued to brief those around me with the information I gave the boss. I also outlined the general plan for the raids.

"Now, I think we need to get introductions out of the way. Keith, I believe you're familiar with everyone. Would you mind introducing everyone?"

"Sure, it would be my pleasure. Everyone, this is Jess. She is currently running lead on this case. She has come directly from the agency's main training facility. Next up is Mini. She is an emphatic healer and water mage. I believe we are all familiar with Gudmundur and Abigail, who are enforcers for the dragon and vampire councils as well as being representatives for their respective councils. We also have Milo, a shifter affiliated with Gudmundur. As for people from the London office, we have Osaki who is a six- tailed kitsune and team leader for one of the strike teams, and Danielle, who is another leader of the London office's strike team. Last of all is me. I am a mage. I mainly work in defensive magic but have some offensive spells when the need requires."

"Thanks, Keith. I appreciate the introductions, but you missed two things. One being I am the girl who was transfused with dragons blood, and a few other things. So if anyone has a problem with that, please speak up now so we can arrange your replacements for these raids." I paused after my statement, giving everyone a steady look. They all met my gaze with amused defiance. "Good, so none of you have a problem working with me on this. The second thing I would like to address would be Danielle. Keith hasn't told us what type of other you are. Are you a vampire, a shifter, a mage, or something else? It isn't my intention to offend you, but I need to know so we can figure out what facility to send your team to." She assessed me with her eyes hardly moving, her breathing shallow, almost predator-like. The silence in the room lasted only a second. "I am a descendant of Melusine, the serpentine lady of French folklore." At the blank look I gave her, she added, "Think of me like a reptile shifter with a little extra thrown in for fun, similar to our kitsune friend Osaki."

Well, that's a turnout for the books. I didn't realise you could be a reptile shifter.

"Okay, thank you. I'm sure that information will prove useful. Osaki, you and your team will have the millennium mills, which is a derelict turn of the 20th-century flour mill in West Silvertown on the south side of the Royal Victoria Dock between the Thames barrier and the ExCel London exhibition centre. The information that Milo has gathered shows that this location is more research than anything else and shouldn't have any live test subjects. It should predominantly have medical researchers and a few security personnel. I think your skills should come in handy. We don't want to set alarms off or draw attention."

"That should be fine. My kind has an affinity for illusions and causing mischief, so we will definitely have the element of surprise, but I will be sure that we won't draw unwanted attention from the public." I could see she glinted with mischief in her eyes. If I got the chance, I would need to spend some time and get to know her when this was all over.

"The next research facility is under Battersea Power Station. The same drill as before, mainly medical researchers, but I think the infiltration will be harder. We have no solid intel, and I can only tell you where the main entrance is. Do I have any volunteers to take this site?"

Danielle spoke up. "I will take this one. With my reptilian affinity, I should be able to gain access without using the main entrance and without alerting anyone. Once I take care of the security and shutdown comms, I can get my team in and secure the site."

Surprised at her willingness to take it on, I just nodded. "Do you need any additional support, or will your team be enough?"

She thought for a moment. "No, I think we should have it handled."

" Okay, next is a testing ground at Abbey Mills Pumping Station abandoned large and retrofitted with cells and medical exam rooms. Milo, I want you to take this one, and Keith, I want you to take the Springfield's Asylum location. Keith, I will also need you to work with Milo on assembling a team while you set up you own infiltration team. Can you both do that for me?"

Both gave me their affirmatives.

"Okay, so that leaves me with the abandoned psych hospital. Mini, I would really appreciate you on this one with me."

"Not a problem. I was kinda hoping you would assign me to this one. I might be able to find something there to help the victims."

"Gudmundur, Abigail. Should I assume that you will be sticking with me, or would you like to lend some muscle on one of the other teams?"

"Abigail and I will stay with you, but I would ask that Alisha stays with Ogma while these strikes take place, and if it is acceptable to you, Aldrich, I have directed a team of dragon breeds and elves to set up a facility outside London to take these victims so they can recover and receive any treatment that will be required." Most of what he said was directed to the screen with the boss and Enlil.

"And who gave the order to arrange this?" the boss asked with a slightly raised eyebrow.

"I made a brief report last night to my queen, and I received this information this morning saying that preparations have commenced. I can notify the work teams to stop if you would prefer to make other arrangements."

"No, that won't be necessary. I would appreciate it if you could pass along my thanks to your queen when you next speak with her."

I could have sworn I could hear a slight tremor of fear in the boss's voice when he said this, but that was in direct contrast to the distinct grins on both Enlil's and Abigail's faces. I have missed something here, and I would find out what it is, eventually.

"Okay, it's now 10 a.m. I want to launch this operation at dusk. Will everyone have their respective teams assembled, recon done on designated sites, and be ready to commence their assaults in that time frame?" They all gave me assurances that they would be ready at dusk and departed to make their individual preparations.

The door closed, and I was faced with Gudmundur, Abigail, and Mini. Even the monitor showing the boss's office had shut down. I slumped back in my chair and started to rub my temples.

"Jess, hun, I can feel what your feelings are, remember? Talk. What has you in such turmoil?"

"Mini, I think something is off. I don't know what, but just something about all of this is wrong. Gudmundur, Abigail, I have a favour to ask. Can we use your people for our infiltration team? I don't know the London teams, and would feel more comfortable if at least someone on our team could trust the people covering our asses."

After a moment of silence, while my statement sunk in, Gudmundur agreed that he would arrange for some teams to meet us at The Dragon's Keep.

***

I thought the team Gudmundur would put together would look a lot like him or even Abigail, but what I was faced with turned out to be team five teams of six people, all of whom looked as though they would give any special op's team nightmares that would have them screaming for their mother.

" I wasn't expecting an army, dragon boy. It looks like you're planning on taking down a small country." "I apologise, but something you said got me airing on the side of caution. Including us, it will be six units hitting this site. One team hitting each side one staying back in a holding formation, prepared to give backup if needed, and a medical team that will work with Mini once the site has been secured."

"Wow." I was impressed. He had got this together a lot quicker than I had thought possible.

"I want it understood that this is my operation, and if any of your people have a problem with what I am, I don't want them coming along. The stakes are high and we all need to be working from the same page. Do I make myself clear?"

Without missing a beat, Gudmundur turned to his people. "Well, you heard the lady. If any of you have a problem with who or what she is, let it be known now, and we can get someone to replace you for this operation." After a few moments of silence, he continued, "We have a lot depending on us doing our job right. We know that the location is going to be heavily defended, and our objectives are as follows. One, subdue all hostile forces with minimal collateral damage. Two, retrieve those being held captive and administer any care required. Three, ensure that they don't get a chance to wipe any of their systems or hard copies of any files. We need to get to the root of what they are doing, why they are doing it, and who is pulling the strings. Is that understood?"

At his question, they all stood to attention and yelled, "Sir, yes, sir!"

"Good, now you all have your assignments. I would just like to say one last thing. They may have aWendigo, so please all be prepared."

Gudmundur, Abigail, Mini, and I left the back area of The Dragon's Keep and made our way to thedining area where we could get some food and talk more about the coming operation. I might be able to grill Gudmundur.

Sat at our table was an assortment of side dishes and a lot of coffee. After Mini had taken in the spread and picked up a cup of coffee, she asked, "So, what's still bothering you? And don't lie to me because your emotions are spoiling my coffee, so out with it."

Mini was good at her job. I could say my emotions were all over the place because of the mission, but I was sure she wouldn't believe me, so I addressed the three of them. "Things aren't adding up. The watcher's council are now taking an interest in what's going on, and that's something I didn't think would happen. The number of big players that are involved in this and the agency is still letting me run point. That's insane. Aldrich's reaction when you said your queen and elves are setting up a recovery site. I need to know what's going on. Are any of you willing to shed any light on the subject?"

Gudmundur was the first to respond. "The watchers involving themselves isn't unheard of, but it is rare, and you're right. With as many people taking an active interest, I would have thought Aldrich would have inserted himself more in the case. As for his reaction to my queen and the elves, well, Aldrich was involved in a very public scandal that involved the dragon breed, and my queen was the one that discovered it and exposed it. He ended up very humiliated, and it has taken a few centuries for him to live down his shame."

"Okay, that kind of explains his reaction, but it couldn't have been that bad if he's now running one of the agency branches."

"It wasn't necessarily illegal, just not really socially acceptable, and it damaged his career. If he wasn't discovered, he could have had Alexander's position on the council and in the agency. The influence that he lost with that indiscretion has haunted him ever since. Just the mention of my queen is enough to piss him off."

"Are you going to tell me who this queen is, or is that some sort of dragon secret too?"

"If what I have been told is correct, she will be at the recovery site, and you will be greeted by her there."

Great, more important people I need to worry about not pissing off.

"Okay, fine. I will put those concerns to the back of my mind for now, but I have something else bugging me. Can you or Abigail set up backup teams at the other raid sites? I have a bad feeling, and I think they are going to need more assistance than they think, but I want discretion. No one is to know that we have arranged back up. If I'm right and there is a mole, us spreading that we have arranged back up could blowback in all our faces."

Abigail rose from her seat. "I will arrange the backup teams. The dragons have already committed enough manpower to this operation. I think it's about time I put some of my resources forward. I agree with what you've said about keeping the information about the backup low key, so I request that I arrange and plan this part of the operation and that I am the only one in the loop until the operation is complete." I agreed with her request but ensured that she understood I would still need her in my team for the actual assault. After hashing out a few last moment details, both the dragon and vampire left me to my thoughts and Mini.

"Mini," I asked, my voice hardly more than a whisper, "do you think this is going to work?"

The only answer she gave me was to pull me into a hug. We sat like that in each other's arms, just silently reassuring one and another that everything would be okay until it was time to commence our attack.

Chapter 17

Infiltrating the facility wasn't as straightforward as we expected. The information that there was a sudden surge of activity was accurate, and that made our job a hell of a lot harder. The site had more security and personnel present than the last time we were here, and it meant we had to overhaul our operation. It looked as though they were attempting to move to a different facility. Files and equipment were being loaded into vans. With a last-minute communication to all the other raid teams, it was decided to hit the cities early. It was going to be crude, and not as well planned as we wanted, but if we didn't strike now, we would miss our chance.

We split the teams so that we could set a blockade up to stop any vehicles from leaving the compound. We also had teams covering the sides and rear of the building to capture any that tried to escape the initial breach at the front of the facility.

I motioned for Gudmundur. "I need you to hit those trucks. Make the attack big and showy; that will get the attention focused on you while Abigail and myself get inside and get a better idea of what's happening, Keep comms open and let us know if you need any backup."

"Okay, should I assume you want to preserve any evidence in the vehicles?"

"Yes, but the lives of the innocents inside take priority. If we lose some evidence and save a life, I'm happy with that."

Gudmundur headed towards the front gate with a grin. "I'm not sure if this is a good idea," I said to Abigail as a huge explosion lit the surroundings and made the earth beneath my feet rumble.

"Well, you did tell him to get their attention." Abigail smirked, trying to hide her laughter.

We waited 30 seconds before we rushed to the front of the facility. Abigail took down the few guards thatstill stood in our way. Once inside, we dove for cover, unsure if we would face any resistance. Whatever Gudmundur was doing was working. As we waited, we saw more guards rush out. After we made sure it was clear, we agreed to separate.

Exploring the building in more detail than the last time, I made sure to check all the rooms. Every one I checked had been ransacked. The areas that had previously had cots filled with people were now bare. Everywhere showed signs of struggle—furniture was overturned, and what looked like blood was smeared on various surfaces. Seeing the blood made me more cautious. I opened my senses up to their fullest and centred myself. With a shudder, I could taste the fear, and smell the blood that had been left to decay over the months and years since this place closed as an asylum. I could also pick up on something fresher, not just fear and blood but hunger, desire, pain and pleasure. I was also starting to feel a wrongness in the energies. It was calling to me like a beacon that I had to follow. I locked onto this feeling of wrongness and headed in the direction it was coming from. I came to a door that lead down.

This is a bad idea, but I know I have to go down there. I clicked my comms unit to get Abigail's attention.

"Jess, what is it? Are you in trouble?"

"Not yet, but I'm heading down to a sublevel, and the energy I can feel is wrong. If you don't hear from me in the next ten minutes, please come looking for me and bring backup if you can."

I waited a moment for her reply. "Abigail, what's wrong? Is there a problem at your end to you need backup? I can make my way to you."

"No, Jess, it's fine. I just might have logistical issues if you need backup. I have come across some survivors and they aren't in great shape, I will try to get them out and come back to assist you, just pleasebe safe."

"Okay, get them out safely and maintain radio contact."

I took another calming breath and head down the staircase. With every step, the feeling of wrongness got more intense. I entered a huge area at the bottom of the stairwell. Back when it was an asylum, it must have been used for storage. Now, it was a place of darkness and evil. The sight of what I was witnessing brought me to my knees, and tears began to wet my cheeks. Chained to the walls were the monstrous forms of half a dozen Wendigos. I thought I understood what to expect when I was told about them, but nothing could prepare me for having six pairs of glowing eyes look over to you. Yellow claws and fangs dripping with blood and saliva, the desiccated flesh pulled tautly over its bones, its stomach distended. The sheer sight of one was enough to inspire nightmares, but six was unspeakable. They were hunched over, all feasting on the bodies scattered around them. It took me a moment to realise that not all the bodies were lifeless. Somewhere, trying to escape, I could see some missing limbs, some gravely injured while others had lost their lives. A look of abject terror was frozen on the lifeless faces.

"Abigail? Gudmundur? Can either of you hear me?" I spoke into my radio and got nothing in reply. I tried them again. "Guys, I need backup and I need it now." Still nothing.

I thought through my options. *I could try to kill the Wendigo and then run for help. I could run for help and hope I get back in time to be some help to the survivors, or I could stay here and defend the survivors until help comes. But how long would that take?*

From a distance, I could hear laughter and the sound of footsteps getting closer. *Looks like my choice has been made for me.* I would need to protect all the survivors that I could. Raising my voice as loud and as commanding as possible, I yelled, "All survivors, make your way to me." I could see that I had startled a few of the survivors, but they started limping and crawling their way closer to me and away from the enemy. I also notice the chains restraining the Wendigo were getting tighter. The monsters were getting dragged towards the walls, away from their prey.

A voice came from the darkness, "So, you made it down here, little girl." I knew that voice, but why couldn't I place it?

"The higher-ups will be pleased to have you back. I couldn't believe it when I heard Jeremiah had been captured and that the great Alexander had taken you in like a lost little kitten." His voice was getting louder and closer as he spoke. He had a crazy gleeful sound to his voice, and I was getting the feeling I wasn't going to like who was behind it

"It took a lot of preparation to set up these

experiments, but any work we lose here, we can recover by studying you. You are my golden ticket. The organisation will be generous with its rewards. I will be set for life, and when we finally make our move, no one will be able to stand in our way. We will no longer hide in the shadows. We will rule the humans, and they will serve us as is their place."

Wow, whoever this idiot is, he definitely has a few screws loose. "Look, I don't care about your master plan, but if you think your life will change, you are massively mistaken. Power and status aren't things that can be given to you. You have to earn them, and people like you with zero backbone will never earn them. You will always be an errand boy. You will always be doing what everyone else tells you because you don't have the brains to think for yourself. Now, show yourself."

"You stupid bitch. I will show that you're nothing more than a failed experiment."

The survivors were behind me now, and I could just make out a figure coming out of the shadows. With him were guards and more captives.

"No, it can't be. You are supposed to be one of the good guys."

Chapter 18

Aldrich exited the shadows with a gun pointed directly at me, a grin plastered on his face. "Alexander and that dragon queen bitch didn't see this coming, did they?" He laughed.

"But I left you at the office with Enlil. How are you here?"

"That blowhard didn't see it coming to either. After you all left, I had my own extraction team take him down. He didn't know what hit him. By the time he wakes up, all this will be long over, and you will be back in our hands and we won't let you escape again."

To highlight his statement, Aldrich fired. His weapon lacked the telltale flash from its barrel that I would expect. I reached up to feel my neck where the round had hit, and I pulled away from a tranquilliser dart. "Son of a bitch, what did you just shoot me with?" My eyes went out of focus, and I stumbled forward, dropping my firearm. There was no point holding on to it. I wouldn't be able to get a clear shot off after being hit with a tranquilliser. I reached for my karambit. Guards began to approach me from behind Aldrich. The pussy wouldn't get his hands dirty. What a shame, well if I was going down I wouldn't goeasily.

The first guard got to me. I was finding it hard to stand, and the room was spinning. The corners of my vision began to blur, completely out of focus. The guard lunged to grab me. I managed to sidestep him and get a glancing strike to his forearm. I could feel my limbs getting heavy, and I had to focus on maintaining my grip on my blades. Whatever they had in those darts was powerful. The spike of adrenaline and the smear of blood on my blade brought everything in to focus for a moment of clarity. I saw more guards bring more prisoners into the chamber, securing a door behind them and making their way towards me. At Aldrich's bellowed instructions to let the Wendigos deal with the failed experiments capture me, the thought of passing out and waking up bound and a prisoner again sent a surge of fear and rage through me. I could feel my blood boiling, my skin felt like a conductor of electricity. I could see an arch of energy crawling over my body ,sparking between different parts of me. My nails started to lengthen and sharpen. I could feel my teeth changing. All of this was happening when I was already in a state of sheer panic and fear was feeding into the power. Surrounding me, the guards that had just moments ago been ordered to capture me now looked at me with a mixture of awe and fear. If I didn't know better, I would say a few were near to pissing themselves.

The only way I can explain this sensation is to say it's like a mix of staring straight at an oncoming tornado and the joy of kissing your first love and feeling truly complete for the first time.

One of the guards raised an mp5 and shot a short burst at my centre mass. The shock took me straight to the ground.

Aldrich's voice rang out. "What do you think you're doing? We need her alive. The boss will kill me if she dies. Get over there and check her vitals and restrain her, even if she looks dead. I want her contained."

Prick can't even bring himself to check that I'm dead. What a loser. But come to think of it, why aren't I dead?

I don't have time to think about it now. I need to stop the Wendigo and make sure the other teams are okay.

A guard lent over me to check my pulse. It was the last thing he did. In a fluid motion, I slit his throat and got to my feet and began working my way through the guards, determined to get to Aldrich and stop this madness before any more lives were lost. With anger still at the forefront of my focus, I concentrated on the combat training I had gone through with Hiyori and Hargreaves. My joints and muscles relaxed, and like a well-oiled machine, I took down my targets with simple, clean efficiency. I turned to blows, then using my opponent's momentum, overpowered them. Disarming and incapacitating was my primary goal, but a few of my opponents wouldn't survive to answer any questions.

With the guards disarmed and unable to come to his aid, Aldrich became scared. I could taste his fear, and I'm not ashamed to admit that I enjoyed seeing him like this.

"So, you want me to meet your boss, Aldrich? Well, how about you tell me where he is and we can all have a nice little chat. Maybe if you have enough information, you will get a reduced sentence."

"You stupid bitch. You really think I'm going to go with you willingly? You don't have enough power to take me down, and even if you did, I'm far too connected to be stuck rotting in prison. No, I think I will see how you compare to my pets. See, the Wendigo here started as test subjects, but now they are my clean-up crew. They are glorified garbage disposal units. Whenever we have no further use for an experiment, we just drop them down here and listen for the screams."

He waved his arm dramatically towards the six monstrosities chained to the wall and, with a snap of his fingers, the chains hit the floor, and they were free. Aldrich went straight for the door as the beasts made a beeline straight for me. I couldn't pursue him as much as I wanted to. I had to protect the victims.

I yelled in a commanding tone, "If any of these get past me and you can fight, defend those around you, reinforcements are on the way."

Still suffering the effects of the tranquilliser, I focused as best I could on the beast heading my way. I dropped all pretences of defensive fighting. I was going to have to go on the attack. I went in low, aiming for the knee joints and the ankle tendons. I needed to reduce their movements as much as possible, and taking them to the ground was my best option. I managed to get in a few good strikes, and one hit the floor yowling in pain. The others had learnt from his mistake and were waiting just out of reach, dodging at my advance.

I was nearly holding my rage and frustration in check. I could feel the Wendigo's hunger and the fear radiating from the survivors. Hargreaves had drilled me a few times on how to do a protection detail, and it was always known where the body was. Next, protect. Usually, that would mean defending, but not against this many, so I needed to keep the attack going. "If any of you can get to the door behind us, check to see if it's open and start evacuating the rest of the survivors," I shouted, hoping someone would follow my instruction.

Just as I had finished speaking, two of the Wendigos took an opportunity to attack. I managed to channel energy to my blades to help boost the overall power of my attack and managed to take off his head. I was a little startled by the result, and the second attacker landed blow to my abdomen. The piercing agony snapped me back to focus, and I blocked the other arm. I pivoted on my right foot, bringing its armbehind its back until I heard the pop of the shoulder dislocating. Hearing its moan of pain was heartbreaking. I continued my attack, bringing it to its knees the then using all the strength I could I thrust my blade in to the base of its skull, killing it and putting it out of its misery. Two dead, one down, and three active targets. I pulled the Wendigo's body from my blade. The three remaining were growling and foaming at the mout,h their eyes showed nothing but primal madness and hunger. *I need to end this, and quick.* From behind me, a timid voice shouted, "The door won't open, and it looks too heavy to break." The voice broke into a sob at the end of her statement.

Shit, well, I will just have to hold out until they find us then. I pulled more power into myself, feeding off the rage, the anger, and the fear that surrounding me/ Alex had said before that if I could manage to harness the dragon part of my power, that what I would be able to do with the surrounding energy would be limitless. Just like earlier, the energy arched across my body. I could feel it in my core and all around me. Reaching out with my mind, I tried to put a dome-like barrier around those behind me so I could focus on the three enemies in front of me. I could feel it taking shape. It wasn't perfect and I was sure it wouldn't withstand a constant assault, but it should deter the Wendigo from attacking them, and they should continue focusing on me. Dropping all my restraint, all my shackles, all the pain, and sorrow that I carried in my heart, the rage and sadness I felt, losing my mother, the anger at myself for the death of my father, the memories of what was done to me in those caves, I let it all out in a concentrated wave of power, but this time, I was in more control. I could feel the strength it was giving me, how my senses became sharper than ever before. My muscles ached, wanting to be used. I felt light as a feather and utterly invincible. The Wendigo resumed their attack, pouncing and lunging at me. I was dodging them with ease and was starting to enjoy myself. Fighting with no restraint, I now understood why paranormals were so arrogant with this much power no one could stand in their way. I became cocky and didn't notice they had begun to herd me to the opposite end of the room and into a corner away from those I was supposed to be protecting. I sliced and cut, my blades like two steel serpents with hungry mouths. It didn't matter how much damage I seemed to inflict on them, they just kept coming. As long as I focused on my anger, I could keep going. I saw nothing but the enemy. I felt nothing, it all melted away into the scent and warmth of blood and sweat.

They wouldn't slow. They kept enclosing in on me.

The fourth Wendigo rejoined the assault, and they became a well-tuned killing machine. They started to land more and more hits on me, and they became more confident. I was boxed in, and I could feel strike after strike. The ground under my feet became slick with blood. I didn't know how much more my body could take, but I pushed on. My arms were becoming numb, and I could no longer raise them to defend myself. My body was covered in slashes and stab wounds from their constant attack. I could see the triumph in the eyes of my attackers—they knew they had won. I dropped down to my knees, no longer able to hold myself up. I had failed. I began to lose consciousness when I heard a *boom*—some sort of explosion had gone off. Maybe the captives would survive after all. The Wendigo continued to attack me, unconcerned with the commotion behind them. I embraced the unconsciousness and the darkness that came with it.

Chapter 19

I was in an unfamiliar bed, unsure of how I got there. I could feel something sticking in my arm, and there was an unmistakable chemical smell surrounding me. My ears were being assaulted by the sound of machinery. In the distance, I could hear the faint sound of a heated discussion. I opened my eyes, finding I was in some sort of medical centre. I had been hooked up to an IV and had monitoring equipment taped all over my body. To finish my look off, I had an oxygen mask on. This was embarrassing, I didn't need all this stuff. I can't have been in that bad a condition,

I decided I wasn't going to stay in bed without any answers, so I pulled the blanket away from my battered body to find that I had been stripped and cleaned. I was also in a fresh set of matching underwear. I really hope Abigail wasn't the one to help put them on me. I blushed to myself at the thought of her teasing me over it. Giving my body a once over before I stood, I could see that 70% of my body was now a stunning combination of yellow, green and purple bruising. It was going to hurt for a while, but it wouldn't kill me. I was also covered in so many deep lacerations across my thighs, chest and stomach. I couldn't stand to count them. Swinging my legs over the edge of the bed, it was time to see if I was strong enough to face the world.

I tentatively put my feet on the ground, being careful not to shift my weight too quickly in case I fell. After a few seconds, I straightened my posture, satisfied that I wasn't about to collapse under the strain of holding myself up. Taking a breath, I removed the monitoring tabs that had been recording my heart rate and blood pressure and other such nonsense. That's when all hell broke loose. Alarms started sounding, doors got slung open and people rushed in. Startled by all the commotion, I stepped back, and this was the point my body decided to betray me and my legs gave out. Looking up at the doctors and nurses who I assumed had thought I had flatlined, or something was also Lyn, Alexander, Gudmundur, and Abigail. Once they saw I was alive and well, the medical team all quickly found somewhere else to be.

Lyn knelt and picked me up from the floor as if I weighed no more than a newborn. With me cradled in her arms, she held me close as though frightened I was going to disappear. After a few tender moments of silence, she placed me back in the bed and pulled the blanket back up to cover the worst of my injuries. "My little dragon, would you like to explain the circumstances that led you to be in this bed?" Lyn said with a firm tone that just screamed that she was pissed. Out of the corner of my eye, I saw Abigail and Gudmundur shift uncomfortably.

I had a feeling this wasn't going to be an easy explanation, but I settled down to tell them what happened. Gudmundur and Abigail were able to fill in details that I couldn't. Apparently, when I was in the sublevel getting my butt kicked, Gudmundur was dealing with magic-enhanced weapons including bullets and explosives. Abigail had liberated a few groups of captives from the upper levels,
but before she could come to assist me, they lost communications.

According to what they told me, the only reason any of us survived in this team was that Alexander, Lyn, and Enlil arrived and took the opposition down with zero resistance. Once they had cleared all the opposing forces, they began to look for me. That's when they picked up on the huge wave of energy I sent out to shield the survivors while I was engaged with the Wendigo. From what the witnesses had pieced together, Lyn was the first one to the sublevel, and she was the one to break down the door. All I was told after that was that I was on the floor, the Wendigo about to finish me off. Lyn flew into a rage.

No one would elaborate any further, but I was assured that the Wendigo were all dead, and after I arrived at the sublevel, no more captives had been killed.

Hearing this report shocked me. I didn't realise that I meant that much to Lyn, and I didn't think I was that close to death. "What happened with the other strike teams? Did the backup we send get to them in time? Did we lose anyone?"

I had to know. It was maddening to think that others may have lost their lives because of Aldrich's betrayal.

Alexander placed a reassuring hand on my leg and said, "Relax, the other sites had been forewarned so they had been more prepared than we expected, but you sending the backup teams saved us from experiencing any fatalities. Some members of the team did get injured, but in time, they will recover. It seems that once it became evident to Aldrich that his plan was unravelling, he chose to shift his focus from hiding his involvement to acquiring you, so he shifted the bulk of his force here, including the Wendigo. I believe he hoped to capture you to give to his boss, or at least that's what the evidence we have recovered indicates."

I nodded at his explanation. "From what he was saying before he left me to die, the organisation that he is a part of was also linked to Jeremiah, and although he didn't come out and say it conclusively, he made it sound as though he as well as others had been to the caves that Lyn and I had been held and that he had seen me and helped take part in some of the tests, but I honestly can't remember anyone other than Jeremiah being there. Do you think he was telling me the truth, or was he just trying to get under my skin so I would lose focus?"

Alex looked at me. "We think after what we've found out today that something much deeper is going on than what any of us had ever thought. We will discuss all of this at a later time, but for the moment, I would ask you to be patient. We need you healthy, because I see a difficult and trying time for all of us going forward," announced Alex.

"Well, about that. I promised Gudmundur and Abigail my assistance with an urgent matter once this case was resolved. But with how things stand, that doesn't seem to be possible. And I think by agreeing to

help them I have also managed to put myself under the authority of a dragon queen I have yet to meet." There was a pregnant pause at the end of my ramblings. All I could think was *shit, I'm in trouble*. Then they all started to laugh. It was like the tension of the past few days had taken its toll on them all. I must have looked confused, because Lyn sat down next to me and said with a smile that everything had been dealt with and I didn't need to worry about anything. She didn't understand. If the dragon queen was a big enough deal to scare Aldrich, I didn't want to get on her bad side. When I made this very reasonable argument, they dissolved into more fits of laughter. I could swear I could see Abigail cry due to laughing so much. At the stubborn look on my face, it must have been obvious I was not backing down, so Lyn took a calming breath. "My little dragon you don't need to fear the dragon queen. She loves you. I can assure you of that." I still didn't understand, so I just blurted out, "Most dragons hate me. So why would she love me? Can someone seriously explain, my head hurts from all this thinking." I then gave Lyn the saddest puppy dog face I could manage. She scooped me into a cuddle and said, "I know she loves you because I am the dragon queen, and I see you as though you're my own daughter. Now, no more questions. You need your rest."

At her statement, I could feel my eyes getting heavy. "Okay, I will take a nap."

I drifted off to a dreamless sleep, listening to Lyn's heartbeat as I lay my head against her chest.

***

In the days that followed Aldrich's betrayal, the paranormal world was in an uproar about all that had happened. All the council representatives called for investigations, certain parties wanted all the victims disposed of when others wanted to study them. After much discussion, it was decided that the victims shouldn't be held responsible for what had been done to them. It was also agreed that the agency would take responsibility for training the victims. This new reality would be a lot to take on, but I knew Ogma was also going to be involved and that reassured me.

I was finally allowed to leave the medical unit after spending what felt like an eternity waiting for the go-ahead from the onsite nurse. I had only just made it outside the medical unit's doo's when an electric pink Shelby Mustang GT 500 pulled up next to me. Slowly, the window rolled down, and I was faced with the

cheery little vampire. "Hello, Abigail. what are you doing here?" I asked, trying as hard as I could to keepmy voice and body language as neutral as possible. I lent down a little more and took a peek inside thecar to find a very grumpy looking Gudmundur in the back seat. I nodded my head at Gudmundur in a subtle hello kind of way, and then turned my attention back to Abigail. "Oh, well, we were just out and about and heard you were being released today, so we thought we would come to pick you up and take you back to the dorms."

"That sounds good. I need to pack and then arrange transport back home."

"What do you mean transport home?" Abigail asked.

"As in me going back to HQ, I need to do some more training and get orders for my next assignment." "You mean you aren't staying at the London office?" Came Gudmundur's voice from the back seat. "Well, as far as I'm aware, I'm getting sent back to HQ, unless you two know more than you're letting on," I said as I got into the car.

Abigail snorted a laugh. "Us? We are far too insignificant to know anything like that, we just thought we would give a friend a ride."

I just shrugged at her. "I'm not falling for that again. I know you both hold a place in your respective councils, and you're both enforcers. But if you don't want to tell me, that's fine. I'll just take a nap while you drive."

They lapsed into a general conversation as I rested my eyes. All too soon, we arrived at the agency's London office. I began to get out. My two shadows unbuckled their seat belts and got out to follow me. "Okay, now what are you up to? Don't try and play innocent with me."

"Well, as you pointed out, we do have official titles, so we are just popping in for a progress update on the state of various investigations, we have no nefarious intentions, I swear!"

"I find that very difficult to believe, dragon boy, but if you're determined to come along, then so be it." I huffed off and entered the building with the dragon and vampire in my wake.

Approaching the desk, I was assaulted in a bear hug from Mini and Keith, both of whom had been waiting to ambush me the moment I came into the building,

Keith was the first to open his mouth. "Well, if it's isn't our great saviour. Come on, the boss wants to seeall of us. I'm guessing you want to see Alisha and Ogma before you get distracted by anything else."

We were taken to what had once been Aldrich's office, but it had been completely cleared and now just held a few comfortable sofas and armchairs surrounding a large coffee table that held an array of snacks and laptops. In the office stood Lyn and Alexander. Both smiled at me and pulled me into their own affectionate hug.

"We apologise that we have not been back to see you, but with everything that has happened, we have been dealing with a lot of fall out. Please be assured that you have never been far from our thoughts. Unfortunately, I will have to rush through pleasantries at this time. Please, can you all take a seat and make yourself comfortable?" Lyn took my hand and lead me to a sofa so we could sit by one another. This behaviour warmed my heart but also scared me slightly.

Alexander cleared his throat. "Thank you, everyone, for coming. I appreciate you all being here on such short notice, but we didn't think this conversation should be had in the absence of Jessica."

At that, Lyn squeezed me in a very reassuring way.

"Everyone in this room is aware of the investigation that has just set the entire paranormal community on edge. We have managed to keep panic to an absolute minimum. But the fact remains that someone has managed to make the head of the London facility betray his own people, conduct forbidden experiments on both the human and paranormal communities, and risked the exposure of the secret existence of the paranormal communities to the world at large. We knew when Jessica and Lyn turned up and we captured Jeremiah that things went far deeper than we wanted. But with the sheer scale of the events that have been uncovered, if we don't get to the bottom of it, well, really, it could destroy the world as we know it. As of now, I am taking control of the London branch. Jessica, Minerva, I am transferring the pair of you to the London branch. This is not a punishment. I would just feel more comfortable with you both near me while we try to unravel the true scope of everything that is happening. I would also like to introduce you to two of the three new hires we have made, I would like to introduce agents Abigail and Gudmundur. They have resigned from their respective positions on the paranormal councils and will be

taking up positions as both lesions and active agents. These two as well as the third will be joining a team that's sole purpose will be to discover how deep these things. Jessica, Minerva, and Keith, you will also be a part of this team. Now, if all that is understood, I would like

Ogma to join us with the other new recruit."

Alexander pushed the intercom button. "Please come in, we are ready for you now."

A few minutes later the door opened and in walked Ogma and DCI Duncan Lancaster. I looked to Lyn and asked, "What's going on? Why is a police officer joining this discussion?"

Lyn just gave me a knowing smile and said, "Be patient, and everything will be explained." I huffed and sat down, watching events unfold.

Alexander stood to greet the new arrival. "Welcome, Mr. Lancaster. Please, come in and sit. I hope you have found your tour with Ogma to be quite enlightening,"

"It has been interesting, but everything I have heard and been told is a lot to take in. From what Ogma has told me, normal people like me don't usually get to know about all of this. So why have you brought me here?"

"You are very perceptive. I would like to offer you a transfer. I would like you to join the agency and be a part of Jessica's team. They will be tracking down leads to apprehend anyone who was connected to the missing persons you have been investigating. Are you interested in seeing this out to the end, or are you just going to walk away?"

Printed in Great Britain
by Amazon